Praise for th

"In the Abigail books, Betha[...] family's commitment to their shared faith can help a nine-year-old girl navigate the everyday problems that children face. Each book not only tells a clever, funny story about Abigail but also successfully unpacks the biblical truths that Abigail discovers along the way."

Bob Hartman, Author and Storyteller

"Bethany has created a delightful series that helps young readers connect their faith with their everyday life. Abigail's adventures are fun and relatable, delivering valuable lessons for all kids and making this series a great one to add to your bookshelf."

Laura Wifler, Cofounder, Risen Motherhood

"Delightful. Relatable. Entertaining. Accessible. True. I am so eager to introduce *Abigail and the Big Start Over* to all of my elementary-aged friends so that they too can adventure with Abigail, identify with her, and discover the incredibly beautiful and immensely applicable power of the gospel in their own very real lives, right alongside her. These stories about Abigail will doubtless impact the stories of their readers in a powerful way."

Abbey Wedgeworth, Author, Training Young Hearts series

"Bethany McIlrath truly understands how to construct an easy-to-connect-with narrative around a gospel-rich passage! Kids who read about Abigail will be entertained, feel understood, and, most spectacularly, come away better equipped to press God's good news into their everyday lives."

Caroline Saunders, Author, *Kids in the Bible*

"Abigail wants to be perfect like Jesus, but she keeps failing. This book will help girls see that you don't have to be perfect to make God proud. My favorite part was when Police Officer Dave saved Abigail from falling off the monkey bars!"

Adelaide, age 9 (review for *Abigail and the Career Day Catastrophe*)

"It was REALLY good. I like how Abigail is trying to impress God and then she realises that she doesn't need to. God just loves her anyway. It was a reminder that you don't have to earn God's love. He's always proud of you."

Jess, age 9 (review for *Abigail and the Career Day Catastrophe*)

"I love this book! It has been the most relatable chapter book I have read to my daughter. It portrays the struggles, conflicts, and pressure that Christian 9-10-year-old girls face. I hope the author writes many more books like this one."

Amazon.com review for *Abigail and the Big Start Over*

"Christian children's novels can be really preachy, but this was great! The author incorporates Abigail's church experiences and thoughts about God into the story in a very natural way, and through this, she represents the lives of her readers. It's wholesome and fun."

Amazon.com review for *Abigail and the Big Start Over*

"My 7-year-old read this chapter book in one sitting from start to finish. Then, she brought it to school to read during free time. This story contains a unique kind of humor which appeals to children, but also adds in Christian values through the biblical principles taught. We can't wait for the rest of the series to come out."

Amazon.com review for *Abigail and the Big Start Over*

Abigail Gets LEFT OUT

Written by
Bethany McIlrath

Illustrated by
Katie Saunders

thegoodbook
COMPANY

Abigail Gets Left Out
© Bethany McIlrath, 2025.

Published by:
The Good Book Company

thegoodbook.com | thegoodbook.co.uk
thegoodbook.com.au | thegoodbook.co.nz | thegoodbook.co.in

With the exception indicated below, all Scripture references are taken from the Holy Bible, New International Reader's Version®, NIrV®. Copyright © 2014 Biblica, Inc.™ Used by permission of Zondervan.

All rights reserved. Except as may be permitted by the Copyright Act, no part of this publication may be reproduced in any form or by any means without prior permission from the publisher.

Bethany McIlrath has asserted her right under the Copyright, Designs and Patents Act 1988 to be identified as author of this work.

Illustrated by Katie Saunders | Design and Art Direction by André Parker

ISBN: 9781802541397 | JOB-007970| Printed in India

Contents

1. Flora's Surprise — 7
2. Can't Sing, Can't Dance — 15
3. Kids' Club — 24
4. Feeling Weird — 33
5. Perfect Love — 41
6. Help Needed — 50
7. Abigail the Sturckle — 57
8. Problems — 63
9. Sturckled Again — 71
10. Wonderfully Made — 80
11. The List — 91
12. Uninvited — 100
13. All Alone — 108
14. The Very Best Friend — 118

15. Saturday	128
16. A Little Cheer	136
17. Delia	144
18. Three Surprises	151
19. A Brilliant Idea	158
20. One Week Later	165
21. What Friends Are For	172
A Note From the Author	183
Book-Club Questions	187

⭐ Chapter One
Flora's Surprise

"Okay then, class," Mr. Ukiyo, the art teacher, called out. "Get to work!"

"Want to guess what I'm going to make?" Abigail asked her best friend Flora.

"Umm," Flora replied, drumming her fingers happily on the sheets of tinfoil they'd been given to turn into little statues. "A panda?"

"Good try," Abigail grinned, knowing Flora was thinking of her favorite stuffed toy at home, "but I would need two different colors for that."

"A... house?" Flora guessed. "Or... a flower? Give me a clue!"

"It's a person," Abigail smiled. Flora loved guessing games, and this must be a good one if she needed a clue!

"Your brother! Your mom! Your dad!" Flora began to exclaim, jumping off her stool as she got into the game. "Your grandpa! Your nana!"

"Nope," Abigail laughed, shaking her head as she began to twist and bend and roll the tinfoil. How was she going to make the hair curly? Hmm...

"I give up," Flora exclaimed. "Who is it?"

"You!" Abigail grinned.

"Beeeeest Chica!" Flora cheered, giving Abigail a high-five. Chica was Flora's special name for Abigail.

Flora looked down at her own tinfoil. "I would try to make you too, but..."

"Yours has to be a dancer," Abigail finished for her. She knew all about Flora's secret goal to squeeze something about dance into every single art project she made while she was 9 years old. So far, she hadn't missed a single one!

"I guess I could make *you* as a dancer," Flora smiled, looking thoughtfully between Abigail and the tinfoil. Abigail thought that sounded nice. She didn't take ballet classes like Flora, and she was kind of bad at balancing and stuff, and she hated being on stage... but it was okay to just *imagine* being a dancer!

CRUNCH. CRUNCH.

They twisted and rolled and trimmed and squished and...

"Voila!" Abigail smiled a little later, holding up a little statue of a girl, with tiny bits of tinfoil rolled up as curls on her head. She'd added a tiny metallic flower headband too.

"It's me!" Flora squealed. "And this is you!"

She held up her shiny statue of a girl with straight hair, holding a box in one hand—and arching her other arm overhead like a ballerina. Her legs were bent like she was mid-leap.

"Can you tell it's your Amazing Adventure Box?" Flora asked happily.

"Of course!" Abigail answered, squinting at the rectangle shape the statue held. She imagined her multi-pen and sticky notes inside, all made of tinfoil. "It's so good!"

"Now," Flora smiled, handing Abigail her real Amazing Adventure Box, "let's pose!"

"Ahem." Mr. Ukiyo was walking over to them. He cleared his throat, looking like he was trying not to laugh as Abigail swayed on one foot, trying to balance in a mid-leap pose while Flora stood next to her holding a paint brush like it was a flower.

"Have you become statues instead of making them?" he teased.

HA! Abigail giggled, and relaxed from her pose just before she was sure she would fall over. She held up her statue of Flora. Flora held up her statue of Abigail.

"I see," Mr. Ukiyo smiled. "Well done. But you're not finished yet. Next, please draw a scene to place your statues on or in front of."

"Hmmm," Abigail said, picking up a purple marker pen as their art teacher walked away. "Where should I put you? In a garden?"

"The grandest garden ever, please," Flora said. "Like one from a fairytale. One where music plays all day long and it never rains but the flowers still bloom, and—oooh, doesn't that sound like a song?"

"You could sing it," Abigail said, as she began to draw a garden with as much enchantment as she could imagine. She could just picture Flora there, talking in her energetic, happy way to anyone about anything. Even the flowers would want to listen!

"Da-da-da," Flora hummed softly to herself as she sat on the stool next to Abigail and drew too. Flora was good at singing. Unlike Abigail.

RINNNGGG!

"I guess we'll finish next time," Abigail sighed happily as the school bell sounded. She collected her statue and backdrop to put on the shelf Mr. Ukiyo used for their class projects.

"I was almost done," Flora grinned, holding up her paper. She had drawn lights, a stage, and the backs of the heads of an audience.

BRRR. Abigail shivered. She had such bad stage fright, she didn't even like to imagine her statue being up in front of everyone!

"I put you in a musical," Flora explained, not noticing Abigail's shiver. "Which reminds me, I have a surprise for recess!"

Abigail waited eagerly while Flora paused to put her project up on the shelf.

"So...?" she asked. "What's the surprise?"

"Sooooo... Brianna and Maggie and I were talking on the bus," Flora began, her dark curls bouncing as they headed toward the door to go outside. "And we all watched the same movie this weekend—isn't that crazy? It was all about this musical, and all these people who watched it and how it made them happy..."

"Uh huh," Abigail said, not seeing what this had to do with a surprise at recess.

"Sooooo," Flora said again dramatically, "we

thought we'd spend recess doing a song and dance from a musical too!"

"Oh," said Abigail.

A song-and-dance routine? That was *not* her kind of surprise.

Chapter Two

Can't Sing, Can't Dance

"We just have to pick the best musical and the best song to do," Brianna explained seriously as the girls gathered together. She brushed one of her pretty black braids behind her back.

"I vote something glamorous," Maggie said, flipping her long, blonde hair over her shoulder dramatically as she came up behind them in the grassy spot where they'd stopped.

"Uh," Abigail said, trying to think of anything

to say—anything at all—about musicals. "What are our choices?"

"Well," Flora smiled, "there's *Matilda*! About a girl with magic powers!"

"Or," Brianna said, adding a very proper accent to her already very proper voice, "there's *Mary Poppins*."

"Orrrr," Maggie argued, "we could do *Beauty and the Beast*. And I would imagine wearing a beautiful ball gown."

"You pick, Chica," Flora said to Abigail generously.

"Uh," Abigail said again, still trying to figure out what to say. She'd only seen a musical once, when her cousin Gracie was in one last summer. What was it called again? She should really remember—her Aunt

Linnea had been in charge of the whole thing!

"It doesn't have to be one of those three," Maggie added.

"Of course it doesn't have to be one of those three—that wouldn't be fair," Brianna said, still sounding like a proper grown-up even though she was 9 like the rest of them. "Which musical is your favorite, Abby?"

"Uh," Abigail repeated. "I don't, um, know any musicals, really. So maybe... maybe we could make up something with my Amazing Adventure Box?"

"You two always play with that adventure box thing," Maggie complained, putting her hands on her hips. "We want to play something cool all together."

"Let's just *try* a musical," Brianna said, coaxing Abigail with a voice that made her feel like she was a little kid again. "I think you'll find it fun once you've *tried*. Right, Flora?"

"Well," Flora said, biting her lip as she glanced between Abigail and the other girls. "I mean, Chica, we're just playing. I forgot, you have stage fright, right? But nobody's watching."

"Sure, right," Abigail said, smiling nervously.

She felt even more nervous when they picked a musical called *Frannie* and a song called "The Future." They told her it was about an orphan cheering people up. But Abigail didn't know anything else about that one—and she couldn't just pose and pretend to be good at dancing like she had in art class. These girls wanted to *actually* dance!

"Are you a soprano or an alto?" Brianna asked Abigail.

"Uh," Abigail said, hesitating.

"She means, what kind of singer are you?" Maggie clarified impatiently.

Feeling her cheeks get hot as she admitted it, Abigail muttered, "I can't really sing…"

"Oh," Brianna said abruptly, curling her lip down with a pity face as she glanced at Flora and Maggie.

"Be a backup dancer, then," Maggie offered quickly, "and when we're singing, you just mouth the word 'watermelon' over and over. I learned that in choir for when you forget the words."

"No one will know the difference," Flora reassured her. She began humming the tune of "The Future" happily.

"Okay," Abigail agreed, feeling uneasy at the thought that there would be anyone watching to know the difference. She set her Amazing Adventure Box out of the way and began practicing saying "watermelon" silently over and over. She was sure she could make up a fun game about watermelons... Maybe they could do that later once they'd finished with the dancing.

"Okay, I've got a plan for the first bit of the dance!" Flora declared, wiggling her eyebrows excitedly. "Start with a grapevine..."

Flora's curls bounced as she crossed one foot in front of the other, and the other behind, and kept doing it as she moved to one side. Abigail tried to copy her. One foot there, the next foot there... No, that wasn't it! Abigail tried again, but she got all tangled up, and...

WHAM.

She tripped and landed in the grass, wishing it tasted like watermelon and not like dirt.

"Sorry, I'll go slower," Flora said, grabbing Abigail's hand and tugging her up.

TAP, TAP, TAP—

WHOA!

Abigail stumbled again, this time falling against Brianna, who scolded her and brushed some grass off Abigail's clothes—like she was her mother!

"Maybe," Abigail sighed as her cheeks burned and the girls looked at her pitifully, "I can't sing AND I can't dance either…"

There was silence.

Nobody, not even Flora, tried to tell her she wasn't that bad.

"Weeelll…" Flora said, thinking hard. "I know! You could be the director." She gave Abigail one of her winning grins. "You just tell us if what we're doing looks right or not."

"Okay," Abigail agreed, wanting to make Flora happy but wishing more than anything that she was somewhere else, doing anything else. How was she supposed to know if they were doing the dance right or not?! Especially since they were creating the dance brand new!

She watched as the girls talked and posed and tried out different moves for their dance. How did they all know what a grapevine was? And a chassé? And a box step? There weren't even any boxes!

"Well, how does it look?" Brianna called out, putting her hands on her hips as soon as Flora was done counting to 8 for the millionth time.

"Great," Abigail said, trying to be encouraging.

"YES!" Maggie exclaimed, swinging around to high-five Flora and Brianna as they all giggled and cheered. "Now let's try it while singing!"

"5, 6, 7, 8," Flora counted as the girls all began to boom out a song about the future.

"The stars'll shine
In the future

Bet you everything else
That the future will be bright!"

It doesn't look very bright for me, Abigail thought to herself, sighing. The girls barely looked at her anymore as they danced and sang in harmony.

What AM I looking forward to? she wondered, trying to find a way to cheer herself up. *Kids' club!* she realized. *It's kids' club at church tonight.* All her buddies there would include her!

⭐ Chapter Three
Kids' Club

Walking down the hallway at church, Abigail felt better than she had at recess. In a moment she'd see Emma and Ruth, who were always happy to hang out. And Smarty-Pants Sam, who loved talking about stories and fun facts with her. And Billy, who was... well, he was Billy, but they always had fun together in the end. Plus, their Bible teacher, Miss Shanner, always picked games everyone played—it wasn't like recess, when kids could split off into groups and leave someone out.

Yes, Abigail told herself, at *kids' club I won't feel so weird!*

CREEEAK.

Opening the door to the fourth-grade room, Abigail looked around.

No Emma.

No Ruth.

Billy was on top of the table already, and Miss Shanner was reminding him that that was not allowed.

Smarty-Pants Sam was...

"Hey Abby," Sam said, coming up behind her.

"Oh, hi," she began to say, but she was interrupted by Sam's dad, Mr. Taylor.

"Hello, young Abby," Mr. Taylor boomed. For some reason, he was talking in a voice that sounded like a wise old sea captain. "I'll be joining ye tonight."

"Ye will?" she asked, perking up. Maybe they could all talk like pirates the whole time. That would be fun! Sam's dad was always lots of fun.

"Yup!" he replied merrily, dropping his pirate voice as he explained, "Well, sort of. We're breaking into groups of boys and girls, and I'll be captain of the boys' group."

"Oh," Abigail answered, her shoulders drooping. She glanced around the room again. Where were Emma and Ruth?!

"A few of the girls are out sick, I hear," Mr. Taylor continued, "so your group should be easier! I've got a lot of rascals!"

"Yeah," Sam chuckled good-naturedly, "I bet your group will actually get to play a whole game, Abby. The boys' group will probably be too rowdy to get through one all the way! The average boy is more active than about 69 percent of girls—I read that today."

CLAP, CLAP!

Miss Shanner got everyone's attention, smiling wide as usual, even though Billy was still on top of the table and some other boys were cheering for him.

"Hey, fourth-grade kids' club!" Miss Shanner beamed. "Tonight's going to be special! We're dividing up into boys and girls to start. Girls, head over to the carpet. Boys, your special guest is Mr. Taylor, and you'll meet..."

"In the hallway!" Mr. Taylor exclaimed, putting back on his silly pirate voice to convince Billy and the cheering boys to go with him. "Off the table with ye! Come to the hall, where there's room to roam!"

"Good luck," Miss Shanner laughed, waving a hand at Abigail to follow her to the carpet where the other girls were already sitting.

THUMP.

Billy leapt off the table and landed on both feet, jogging right past Abigail.

"Bet we're going to have more fun than you!" he called out to her happily.

Classic Billy, Abigail thought. Everything was a competition between her and Billy. She won probably half the time. But this time, Abigail realized with disappointment as she looked at the other girls on the carpet, Billy was probably right. He *was* going to have more fun than her—even if the boys didn't behave!

There were four girls besides Abigail, and they were sitting in two pairs, arm in arm.

Already buddied up.

"I'm afraid we're down to 5 tonight," Miss Shanner said, sitting cross-legged on the carpet and patting the spot next to her for Abigail to sit down. "Our other friends are out sick."

SIGH.

Abigail wished Emma was there, cracking jokes and egging her on with her usual "come on" encouragements to join in. She could make anything fun.

Or, if Ruth were there, even though she was shy and barely spoke above a whisper, she'd notice Abigail was alone and stick with her. Ruth was always very nice.

And these girls, well... they weren't mean, but...

The first pair of girls, Maisie and Shia, had been friends since their first kids' club when they were 5, when they'd walked in wearing the same t-shirt with a dog on it and started calling each other "Twin!" They had talked about their dogs for a long time, and Abigail still remembered how she'd tried to join in by telling them about her grandparents' cat, Snickers. But they both said they didn't like cats and went back to talking about the things they had in common. And ever since then, Abigail had been pretty sure they didn't like cats *or* her. They'd never really tried to be her friends.

Glancing from the "twins" to the two other girls there, Abigail felt just as discouraged.

Lucy and Katie were besties too, since they both did gymnastics. Really, all Abigail knew about them was that they always partnered up for games and always wore ribbons around ponytails or buns. They both could do splits and back bends and flips. And, when it was time for prayer requests, they always asked God to make their gymnastic meets or competitions go well. Most of the time, they both wore t-shirts that read "Tumblers Team".

Abigail wasn't even sure what a tumbler was, except that it had something to do with gymnastics. She'd never done gymnastics. She'd never even finished a cartwheel properly!

"Let's all start with a this-or-that activity," Miss Shanner said. "I'll give you two options. Stand up if you'd pick the first one."

The twins whispered something to each other and high-fived. The tumblers gave each other a silent nod with squinty eyes, like there was a game to win and they were going to be victorious.

But Abigail didn't have anyone to nod at or high-five.

She felt just like she'd felt at recess.

SIGH.

⭐ Chapter Four

Feeling Weird

"Vanilla or chocolate?" Miss Shanner asked to start their game, then added, "Vanilla stands."

Abigail stood up, all by herself.

"Oh, fun," Miss Shanner began to say.

"What's next?" one of the tumblers interrupted excitedly. Abigail dropped back down onto the carpet, noticing awkwardly how the pairs of girls kept looking at each other making faces and giggling, the way best friends do.

"Beach or mountain?" Miss Shanner asked, leaping up as she exclaimed, "Beach stands!"

Abigail leapt up again, relieved that this time she was standing right alongside the tumblers.

"Because you can do more gymnastics in the sand," Lucy explained, looking at her friend as she said, "right?"

"Yeah," Katie answered, "exactly!"

"Yeah!" Abigail added, blushing and immediately wondering why she'd said that.

They all sat down again.

"Art class or music class?" Miss Shanner asked. "Art stands!"

Abigail launched onto her feet again, this time next to the twins.

"What kind of art do you like to do?" Miss Shanner asked everyone standing.

"Well," Abigail began to explain, looking at Maisie and Shia and hoping they'd like her more now that they had art in common. "I like drawing, doodling, painting, and coming up with creative stuff. I have an Adventure Central at home where I can draw on the walls, and... I just like art. All art!"

"That's great." Miss Shanner smiled at her before looking between the twins. "How about you two?"

"Ha!" Maisie, one of the twins, giggled.

"We just agreed to stand up for the third question so we could keep twinning," Shia giggled back.

"Yeah, we don't really *do* art," Maisie added.

URRRGGGH.

Abigail heard herself partly groan, partly sigh. Of course the twins didn't like art. They didn't have anything in common with her!

"That's not the game, girls," Miss Shanner

said, shaking her head. "Answer honestly next time, alright?"

"Ooookay," the twins giggled, sitting back down.

Abigail was pretty sure they were just going to copy each other for the next answer too.

"You've done all the standing ones," Miss Shanner commented to Abigail with a grin as she sat down.

"Does that mean something?" Lucy, one of the tumblers, asked, raising an eyebrow competitively. "Like, does she win or lose?"

"No," Miss Shanner said, "it doesn't mean anything really. Just that Abby likes the first options, I guess."

And that I stand out, which is basically losing, Abigail added inside, praying she could stay seated for the next one, whatever it was. And that everyone else would stay seated too.

"Last one," Miss Shanner continued.

"Friends…"—she let her voice get dramatic—"or enemies? Friends stands!"

SIGH.

Abigail got up on her feet, knowing she couldn't stay sitting for that one. Miss Shanner had said to be honest. Abigail loved friends. Who would pick enemies?!

At least everyone else was standing this time too.

"I'm not surprised that no one picked enemies," Miss Shanner chuckled. "See, today we're talking about friendship. And guess what? Even though we all like different things and are very different people, everyone needs friends. God designed us for relationships!"

As the twins hugged each other and the tumblers high-fived again, Abigail looked at her feet, wishing for the second time that day that she was anywhere else, doing anything else.

"Right, let's move to the tables for our lesson," Miss Shanner said hurriedly.

Phew, Abigail thought to herself. She was so ready to be done with their game—and to be done with standing out.

But the twins rushed to sit at one of the two tables together... and the tumblers sat at the other, their matching hair ribbons making them look very official.

Where do I sit? Abigail wondered, feeling out of place. She'd never even had to think about it before! Ruth, or Emma, or Sam, or Billy always had a spot next to them, and at least one of them always wanted her in it!

GULP.

Slinking towards the tables as if going slow would make her embarrassment invisible, Abigail sat down as silently as she could next to the tumblers. They might not notice her, but at least they didn't make it obvious that they didn't like her, like the twins did.

"Before I give you today's papers," Miss Shanner said, "does anyone know the Bible memory verse?"

Normally, Abigail would have shot her hand up as fast as she could to be first and to beat Billy in their forever-everything competition. But this time, she didn't really want to feel like all the other girls were looking at her. Even if she did know the Bible verse by heart already.

...

...

...

"No one?" Miss Shanner asked.

Abigail could practically feel Miss Shanner's greenish eyes staring at her, but she didn't look back.

"Okay, it is: *Here is my command. Love one another, just as I have loved you.* John chapter

15, verse 12. That's Jesus speaking, telling us to love each other like he loves us."

Abigail's heart ached a little. She hadn't felt very loved that day.

Jesus said, "Here is my command. Love one another, just as I have loved you." John 15:12

Who do you want to love with Jesus's love?

Draw them or write their name here:

⭐ Chapter Five

Perfect Love

"Who likes to be loved?" Miss Shanner asked.

Everyone stuck their hands up.

"And who keeps this command?" Miss Shanner asked. "Do any of you love others the way Jesus loves—perfectly?"

HA! Over on the twins' table, Maisie wiggled her hand like she was "so-so" at loving like Jesus. Shia giggled.

Abigail didn't laugh. She didn't think it was funny, not when those girls had never been very loving to her.

"Well," Miss Shanner said, raising an eyebrow at the twins, "here's the thing about loving others like Jesus—it's hard. Even if we *want* to be loving at all times, we aren't perfect. So even though relationships are such good gifts from God," Miss Shanner continued, her voice getting gentle, "sometimes even the people closest to us disappoint us. And we disappoint them."

ZINNNG! Abigail felt a sting in her heart so strongly she could swear something was poking her. "Sometimes even the people closest to us disappoint us." That was Flora! Abigail had always been able to count on her enthusiastic, curly-headed friend. But today at recess Flora hadn't even noticed that Abigail felt left out.

"Here," Miss Shanner said, handing out a paper with the Bible verse on it. "I hope you'll memorize this verse. Partly because it reminds us of what our friendships *should* be like and the kind of loving people God wants us to be—

but also because it reminds us that we need a Savior."

Jesus is the Savior, Abigail thought to herself. She knew that already. But she wasn't sure what Jesus being the Savior had to do with a friend like Flora disappointing her so badly.

SQUEAK, SWOOSH, SQUEAK!

Miss Shanner went to the whiteboard and wrote "God" and "People" on it, close together in a circle.

"God designed people to be close to him, and to love him and love each other," Miss Shanner explained as she pointed to the circle. "But when we sin, what do you think that does to the relationship between people and God?"

"SPLITS them apart," Lucy said. "Like a split in gymnastics," she added, glancing at Katie with a giggle.

Miss Shanner nodded. "We can't be close to God anymore because of our sin."

She erased the circle with God and People written in it.

"And," she explained, "when we sin, it splits us apart from other people as well. We all hurt each other sometimes. Sometimes on purpose, sometimes without meaning to. Even our best friendships have brokenness because of sin. So now, this is what our relationships look like…"

SQUEAK, SQUEAK.

Miss Shanner wrote the word God again at

the very top of the board. At the far left-hand side she wrote People and at the far right-hand side she wrote Other People.

Now everyone was far apart from each other.

SIGH. Abigail knew what it was like to feel all alone.

"But remember how I said our Bible verse reminds us we need a Savior?" Miss Shanner asked, raising her eyebrows. "We can't fix this problem of sin on our own. We need someone to fix what's broken! And... someone can! Someone does!"

Abigail took a deep breath, feeling some hope.

"Jesus!" Miss Shanner cheered.

SQUEEEAAAK.

She drew a long vertical line from God at the top of the board all the way to the bottom.

"Jesus came down to save us. He helped SO many people—he was a friend to the lonely, he cared for the sick, he listened to people everyone else ignored! Then he died to take away our sin and came to life again so that, if we trust in him, we can be close to God again."

Grinning, Abigail thanked God in her heart for Jesus. Even if other people didn't love her perfectly, she knew he did!

"Aaaand," Miss Shanner continued after a dramatic pause and deep breath.

SQUEEEAAAK.

She drew a line from side to side between People and Other People. The two lines looked like a cross! *Because Jesus died on a cross to take away our sin and make everything alright again,* Abigail realized.

"Jesus helps us in our relationships with each other too. One day, he is going to make everything new and right, and then it will be easy to really love each other and love God!" Miss Shanner exclaimed. "And until then, we can ask Jesus to help us love one another better, and he will."

YAY! All the girls cheered. Abigail felt warm inside as she saw Lucy and Katie smiling at her.

Thank you, God! Abigail prayed, grateful that Jesus loved her AND that Jesus helped people love each other AND that the tumblers had actually included her!

"Jesus loves us perfectly," Miss Shanner finished, holding up one of the Bible memory papers. "He is THE best friend we could ever have. And he helps us to love each other just as he has loved us. So... I have a project for you all! This week, we're going to love as Jesus does by serving others. We're going to make cards to encourage people who are feeling lonely in a nursing home."

WOW! Abigail couldn't help gasping with excitement. Making cards sounded awesome! She could do art, and write nice things, and help others—and Flora was great at cardmaking, so maybe she'd want to help with that instead of doing the musical again!

"Abigail's nana is going to pick up the cards from each of you on Friday night and then deliver them on Saturday morning," Miss Shanner finished explaining as she handed out the blank, folded pieces of paper. "You can start on the cards now, or make them at home."

Abigail beamed. She loved Nana, and she

loved how she and Grandpa were always helping people!

"That's cool of your nana to deliver the cards," Lucy said, smiling again at Abigail and shuffling her chair a little closer.

"Yeah!" Katie agreed. "She must be really nice, like you."

"Thanks," Abigail beamed even bigger, feeling full of love and hope suddenly.

"Hey, want to do tumbles with us?" Lucy asked her kindly. "We can teach you!"

"Umm, I might be bad at it..." Abigail replied, remembering how recess had gone.

"So?" Katie shrugged. "Everybody is bad at stuff until they practice."

"Let's go!" cried Lucy. The tumblers high-fived each other. And then they high-fived Abigail!

Chapter Six

Help Needed

Taking a deep breath as she walked into her classroom at school the next day, Abigail said a prayer in her head. *Jesus, please help me have good relationships today! Like Miss Shanner said!*

"Hey, Chica!" Flora called out, waving at her from the back of the classroom where there was a little free space near a bookshelf. "I need your help!"

"And I need YOUR help!" Abigail answered back hopefully, tugging out of her backpack the blank cards she'd brought to make for the lonely old people in the nursing home.

"Mrs. Hennig saw us dancing and told us if we want to, we can show the *whole class* our song and dance from *Frannie*! She said we can do it on Monday after recess!" Flora explained, bouncing excitedly. Maggie and Brianna lined up on either side of her.

"It's going to be so *elegant*," Maggie said, drawing out her last word, which Abigail thought must be her favorite.

"But we can't decide which dance sequence to start with," Brianna explained.

Abigail's shoulders slumped a little and she gripped her cards tighter. She'd hoped the girls would want to play something other than musical! And now... now they weren't even just playing. They were practicing for real!

"Help us pick!" Flora said happily as she nodded at the other girls to begin their steps. "5, 6, 7, 8," she counted.

Abigail wondered what had happened to the first four numbers.

SHUFFLE

    TWIRL

        WIGGLE

            STOMP.

"That was version 1," Flora smiled as the three girls paused. "Now here's version 2…"

SLIIIDE

    STEP, STEP

        SLIIIDE

            SPIN!

"So which one is better?" Maggie asked Abigail, straightening her already straight skirt just to make it extra perfect.

"Uh," Abigail said out loud. She had no idea which dance was better. What was the difference anyway? She glanced down at the blank cards in her hands like they might tell her what to do. They reminded her of kids' club, and the tumblers and... **DING DING DING!** It was like a lightbulb went on in Abigail's head. She suddenly had an idea that would make her more a part of the whole thing!

"How about adding a tumble?" she suggested in her best director voice. "That will make the dance REALLY stand out."

"I'm not sure—" Brianna began to say, scrunching up her face.

"I'll show you," Abigail interrupted, praying inside that she had practiced enough to do the front roll tumble that Lucy and Katie had taught her the night before.

"We know what a tumble is..." Maggie began to explain.

But Abigail wasn't listening. She was remembering how the hard part of a front roll was not using her hands to catch herself and get up.

She set down her blank cards.

She squatted down on the floor.

She bent... rolled...

ROCK...

    ROCK...

        ROCK...

Nope. She was stuck!

Quickly using her hands to get up, Abigail tried to look brave. Maybe she hadn't gotten it exactly right, but she'd proved she could be a good director, at least!

"Um, yeah, so," Maggie said, dusting off her perfectly clean skirt, "we're going to wear dresses for costumes and stuff... which we don't want to get dirty."

"It wouldn't be ladylike to roll in a dress, especially in front of an audience," Brianna added sagely. "I was on TV once when I was little, and that was an important rule."

"It was a good idea though," Flora said, giving Abigail a grin that looked like it was hiding a grimace. Abigail thought Flora's cheeks maybe even looked a little red.

"Okay," Abigail said, fighting to keep her voice steady. Her tumble was a fail. Her being part of the musical at all was a fail. And Flora—her best friend—was embarrassed by her! That felt like the biggest fail of all.

"We can decide about the dance later, anyway.

Let's plan our costumes and makeup," Maggie said, shrugging off the tumble kerfuffle. "I'm Frannie, so I'll need to find a red wig. Unless my mom lets me dye my hair. Hmm. Probably not. I'll have to beg just for makeup!"

"Mothers..." Brianna rolled her eyes.

Abigail thought it was a bit silly for Brianna to be annoyed about mothers, since she always acted like one.

"But there are only a few minutes before the bell rings," Brianna pointed out, tapping her wrist like she had a watch, even though she didn't. "We'd better practice again, my little stars."

Chapter Seven

Abigail the Sturckle

Flora, Maggie, and Brianna lined up and began their moves again.

"Step here," Brianna said, pausing their dance a few times to correct them, "a little faster."

SIGH.

Abigail picked up her blank cards and bit her lip.

She kept her eyes on the floor and away from motherly Brianna's "little stars," since she wasn't really one of them. They weren't even asking her for director-type advice since the tumble fail. There was nothing for her to do except go away.

Hearing Flora count out "5, 6, 7, 8" again, Abigail sighed louder and turned to slink off to her desk.

This is going to be so embarrassing! she moaned inside. *Everyone knows me and Flora are best friends. So, when she does the musical and I don't*

have any part in it, they're going to know I wasn't good enough! They'll probably think she's picked better, more talented friends! And maybe... maybe she has.

She glanced back over her shoulder as she walked away and saw Flora's wide, happy smile. It was like she hadn't even noticed that Abigail had gone!

BUMP.

"Woah, watch out," Greg said, stepping back as Abigail walked into him. He was her friend, well, some of the time. It depended if he was teasing too much.

"Sorry," she sighed, feeling tears prickle at her eyes.

"What's wrong? Did you hit your head on the floor or something?" Greg asked.

"Huh?" Abigail was confused.

"When you were rocking there—being a stuck turtle or whatever you were mimicking, did you hit your head?" he explained.

"We were, uh, practicing a dance," Abigail replied, feeling her cheeks grow hotter than they had even when she kept messing up in front of the musical girls.

"Really?" Greg snorted, apparently not worried about her head anymore. "You looked like a stuck turtle, a s-turtle. Or, no... a sturckle!"

Abigail's cheeks were on fire. She whipped away from Greg.

SNIFFLE!

She just didn't fit in! Not with Greg and his sometimes-friend, sometimes-too-much-teasing ways. Not with Brianna and Maggie, who could sing and dance and always had their hair just right. Not with Flora, who'd forgotten all about her and was embarrassed by her, even!

Please, Jesus, she prayed in her head at her desk as she stared at her blank cards, trying not to cry, *Miss Shanner said that you'll help us have good relationships. And I want to, but... nobody wants to be my friend!*

RINNNGGG!

Abigail tried to rub the red and teary look from her eyes before Greg sat down at his desk next to her for math. She did NOT want to have to explain tears to him. He'd probably make a joke about a wet sturckle or something.

"Alright, class," Mrs. Hennig said before anyone else had had a chance to sit down, "We're going to do some partner work during math. Please get into pairs and help each other if you get stuck on any problems."

GULP.

Abigail turned

around to find Flora—they were always partners. But Flora's smile turned to meet someone else's instead.

Maggie.

She'd grabbed Flora's arm and was already tugging her back toward her own desk.

"But!" Abigail began to protest, feeling tears well up again even though she tried to hold them back. She and Flora were ALWAYS partners! Everyone knew that!

"Don't worry," Brianna interrupted, coming up behind Abigail on the other side. "We'll be partners today."

"Oh," Abigail answered, worrying a lot more inside. She had never been partners with Brianna before. Brianna and Maggie were besties, just like she and Flora were. Or... maybe like she and Flora *used* to be.

⭐ Chapter Eight

Problems

"Are you okay? Your face looks red. Maybe you should go to the nurse," Brianna said worriedly, placing the back of her hand on Abigail's forehead before taking Greg's now empty desk next to her. "I think you're warm. I hope you don't have to go to the hospital. Hospitals are scary!"

"I'm fine," Abigail lied, sniffling as silently as she could. "I just…"

What could she say?

"You don't like math, is that it?" Brianna

asked knowingly, interrupting again. "I noticed. You know, you never raise your hand during math. Lots of kids don't. Don't worry. I'm good at it. I'll teach you."

Abigail couldn't even muster up a thank-you. She wasn't even sure she wanted to. Did everyone in the class know she was bad at math? Was it that obvious?

RUSTLE.

Mrs. Hennig hurriedly pulled two sheets of paper from the stack she was carrying and handed them to Abigail as she walked between the rows of desks.

"I'll get us going," Brianna said, not even waiting or asking politely as she took both papers from Abigail and glanced them over before handing one back to her. "Here's yours."

"Are they the same?" Abigail asked, glancing from one sheet of math problems to the other.

"No," Brianna explained, pointing to the bottom of her paper where there was a number 2. "See? I have page 2 since it looks harder, and once I've finished it, I'll help you with page..." She pointed at the number on the bottom of Abigail's paper.

"1," Abigail answered, bristling at the way Brianna bossed her around but acted like it was for her own good. "I *can* count."

"Sure," Brianna replied absently, her eyes already back on her own desk. Abigail watched as Brianna scrunched her face up and concentrated on the problems in front of her, her pencil poised over the paper.

I guess Brianna isn't a "hang out together" kind

of partner, Abigail sighed inside.

She glanced behind her to look for Flora, wishing they were together instead. Flora was smiling and giggling as she and Maggie gestured at each other's hair and clothes while they talked and nodded at each other's worksheets. With their big smiles, they made math look like fun.

"Don't worry, Abby, I'm almost done," Brianna said, as if Abigail needed to be watched over. She was still scratching away with her pencil on her paper.

Staring at the worksheet in front of her, Abigail squinted. She smiled. She tossed her tangly hair over her shoulder, trying to make herself feel as happy to be doing math as Flora and Maggie looked.

THUMP. Her headband slipped off, onto the desk. She was pretty sure it took all the numbers in her brain with it.

Math might be fun for some people, but it definitely wasn't for Abigail. As she tried to work out how to solve even one of the math problems in front of her, she didn't just feel bored. She felt stupid—especially since her quick glances at Brianna's paper showed she really was almost done. Brianna must be *very* good at math.

"So, let's see how far you've gotten," Brianna said, leaning over to take a look at Abigail's paper. "Oh, you haven't started. Do you know where to start on this type of problem?"

"Yes," Abigail lied. Probably she *could* figure it out if she weren't feeling so hot and sad and alone and stupid—and stuck! Like a sturckle.

With Brianna hovering like a mother hen, and the sound of Maggie and Flora's giggles behind her, Abigail couldn't actually think what to do. She couldn't think of anything except how bad she was at so many things!

"Here," Brianna said, standing to be as near to Abigail's desk as she could. "Just watch, I'll show you."

SCRITCH, SCRATCH.

Using her own pencil on Abigail's paper, Brianna began to write down a number and explain some gobbledegook about carrying a numeral here and dividing something else there.

All Abigail heard was a voice inside that said, *You're no good at anything.*

That voice only got louder when Mrs. Hennig came by to collect their papers just as Brianna finished doing Abigail's for her, still chattering away about what do with those numerals.

"Abby," Mrs. Hennig said to Abigail as she picked up her paper and glanced between it and Brianna's. "Did Brianna do your work for you? It was meant to be a partner exercise."

"Oh, it's okay," Brianna assured Mrs. Hennig before Abigail could say anything. "I was helping her out since math isn't really her thing."

"That's nice of you," Mrs. Hennig said flatly, as Abigail's cheeks flushed and she bit her lip, trying not to argue that it somehow didn't feel very nice actually, and she hadn't asked for the help. Mrs. Hennig straightened her pointy glasses and explained, "But Abby needs to do her own work and ask me for help if she's having this much trouble. Abby, I'll need to keep you inside during recess to practice these problems with me."

SIGH.

"Okay," Abigail agreed, hardly above a whisper.

"Yikes," Brianna said, moving to return to her desk as soon as Mrs. Hennig walked away. "Sorry, Abby. Don't worry, though. Keep practicing. You'll get there! And I'll tell the other girls so they don't worry about you when you miss recess."

Great, Abigail groaned inside. *Just great.*

⭐ Chapter Nine
Sturckled Again

"Hey, Chica!" Flora exclaimed, bounding up to Abigail as soon as she and Mrs. Hennig stepped out into the bright sunlight to call the rest of the class inside. It was time for lunch and Abigail had been stuck inside for all of recess.

"I missed you!" Flora cried.

"You did?" Abigail asked, suddenly

feeling hopeful. Maybe Flora was still her best friend! Maybe they could make the cards from her Amazing Adventure Box at lunch.

"Sssh!" Mrs. Hennig reminded them to be quiet in the hallway.

SHUFFLE, SHUFFLE, SHUFFLE.

The class walked toward the doors to the cafeteria. Mrs. Hennig held one open so they could get in the lunch line or find a table if they had a packed lunch.

"Do you have your lunch already? Want to get us a table while I wait in the line?" Abigail asked Flora, wondering if she should offer for Brianna and Maggie to join them.

"Oh, sorry, Chica," Flora answered, stopping before she stepped through the doorway and glancing back over her shoulder at Brianna and Maggie. "When Mrs. Hennig asked us about performing, she also said we could eat lunch in the classroom so we could get in more practice."

"Ready, girls?" Mrs. Hennig asked, beginning to close the cafeteria door.

"See you later!" Flora called out cheerfully.

CLANNNG!

The door shut, and Abigail stood there staring at it.

"Are you a sturckle again?" Greg joked, tapping her shoulder.

"What?" she asked, trying not to let tears well up again. Flora had forgotten her that morning. Maggie had stolen Flora during math. Brianna had got Abigail stuck inside during recess. And now she was all alone for lunch?!

"Hello?" Greg said, tapping her shoulder again. "Are you a sturckle or what? The line is moving."

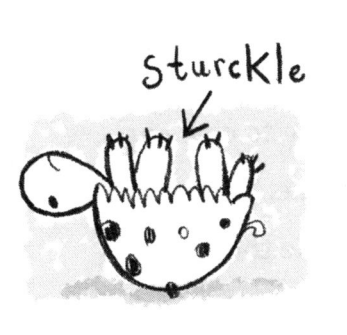

"Oh," Abigail answered, looking down at her shoes and the row of

73

shoes in front of her as kids shuffled through the lunch line. She followed Greg's red sneakers and collected her tray and food like she did every day. Except today she felt like a robot with its heart ripped out. Wasn't that a movie or something? Or... a musical?

SIGH.

"What's your problem?" Greg asked as Abigail followed him to a table.

"Nothing," she said. He wouldn't understand!

"Well, okay," Greg shrugged. "Want to play a game or something?"

"What game?" Greg's friend Ian asked from across the table.

"Uh," Abigail said, quickly taking a bite of her sandwich and thinking. She glanced at her Amazing Adventure Box, trying to come up with an idea the boys would like. They probably wanted something fast, not like the guessing games or stories she and Flora liked best. "How about... uh..."

Greg opened his mouth, and Abigail just *knew* that if she kept pausing, he was going to make another sturckle joke!

"How about turtle tag?" she asked as quick as she could, trying to beat Greg to any turtle-type talk.

"What's that?" Greg asked, raising an eyebrow.

"We, uh..." Abigail answered, pulling out some sticky notes and her multi-pen as she tried to make up the game fast, "we draw a turtle's top half on one side of a sticky note and its bottom on the other and uh..."

"Haha!"

Greg was laughing at the word "bottom." But Abigail didn't mind. She was too busy having fun making up the game.

"We slide them all around the table, two at a time. You can't stop moving your turtle, and you can't lift it off the table! If you can get your turtle to slide over the top of the other turtle, you win that round. The other turtle has to be flipped over because it's out. Then the next two turtles play."

Abigail looked around the table, hoping the game made sense.

"Okay," Ian shrugged at Greg.

"Sure," Greg shrugged back, nodding at the other kids around them.

Abigail handed out sticky notes and everyone took turns drawing their turtle tops and bottoms between bites of lunch.

"Let's do it," Greg finally said, just as Abigail finished her drawing and stashed her multi-pen away.

SWOOSH, SWOOSH!
THUD.

"Hey!" Ian exclaimed as his turtle got flipped.

"Yeah, yeah, take that," Greg said, slamming his turtle on top of everyone else's as he flew his in the air like a bird. That was against the rules! And he hadn't even let anyone else have a turn!

"Hey!" other kids called out, racing to pick up their turtles and slam them into each other as crumbs flew everywhere. Abigail watched, biting her lip.

"If turtles can fly," Ian argued, "then watch out!"

WHOOSH...
SMACK!

Ian wadded up his sticky note turtle into a ball and tossed it at Greg's face.

WHOOSH... WHOOSH...
SMACK! SMACK!

Other kids joined in, laughing.

Greg laughed too, scooping up as many balled-up sticky-note turtles as he could and hurling them back.

"This game is way better," Ian said.

"Yeah, this game is actually fun!" Greg echoed, "I call it... dodge turtle!"

"Yeah! Yeah!" the other kids exclaimed as sticky notes flew all over the place.

"But..." Abigail tried to say over their noisy, messy, not-nice game. She gave up. She had liked her turtle tag idea. She had liked when they all were listening to the rules and talking about her idea and playing it the right way. But now no one was listening, and no one was noticing that she was trying to speak, and her game was wrecked, and she wasn't going to play this turtle-crushing craziness that a teacher was DEFINITELY going to come and tell them to stop.

WHACK!

"What's wrong?" Greg called out as he tossed one of the sticky-note turtles at her face. "Are you a sturckle again?"

Yes, Abigail thought to herself sadly, ignoring him. *Sturckled all alone, sturckled bad. Just sturckled.*

Chapter Ten

Wonderfully Made

"Hen-hen-Henry!" Abigail called out as soon as she burst through the front door at home. She couldn't wait to hear him say his nickname for her in his little toddler voice. He always called her Gabigaa. Sometimes, she hated it. Other times, that silly loving name made her feel like she belonged. And she really wanted to feel like she belonged right now.

But there was no reply.

•••

•••

•••

Silence.

"Mom?!" she called out next.

Mom's hand waved around the corner of the kitchen doorway.

"Mom... where's Henry?" Abigail asked, walking into the kitchen.

"Hang on," Mom answered, tapping the mute button on the phone she was holding. "Hi, honey—Henry's at a friend's house. I'm on the phone with Aunt..."

"Aunt Linnea?!" Abigail interrupted. If anybody could help her figure out what to do about this musical thing, her theatre-director aunt could!

"Auntie Louise," Mom finished. "You can say hi in a few minutes, okay?"

Abigail smiled. She didn't know if Auntie Louise knew anything about musicals. But she would definitely understand all Abigail's tangled up, embarrassed feelings. Auntie Louise and Abigail were a lot alike. Abigail was even named after Auntie Louise, whose middle name was Abigail! Auntie Louise *always* understood, even though she and Uncle Thomas and Cousin Evangeline lived far away and they almost never saw each other.

"Can I talk to her now?!" Abigail asked, just wanting someone to make her feel okay inside.

"In 10 minutes."

Mom turned away, unmuting the phone.

"But Mom!" Abigail protested as loudly as her

feelings felt. "Can't I just talk to her now?!"

"In 10 minutes," Mom began to answer. "We're in the middle of—"

"HI, AUNTIE LOUISE!" Abigail yelled anyway, thinking she might burst if she had to feel left out a minute longer that day.

"Sorry, hang on," Mom said into the phone before shooting Abigail a look. "Abby, I said 10 minutes."

"I can't wait," Abigail argued.

"Yes, you can," Mom said.

"But..." Abigail protested.

"Abby," Mom said seriously, "I will let you say hi in 10 minutes."

"But *why?!*" Abigail whined, stomping her foot a little. She knew she was acting like a little kid. But she'd had a bad day, and she didn't want to keep being left out of things!

"Sorry, be right back," Mom said into the phone, tapping the mute button fiercely. "Abby, what is going on with you?!"

"Everything! Everything is going on!" Abigail burst out, feeling horrible and frustrated and guilty and selfish and all sorts of other ugly things inside. "You don't understand! Nobody wants to talk to me or play with me or... And I'm not good at dancing! Or singing! Or math! People don't like my games! I'm not good at anything! And nobody wants to include me!"

"Abby!" Mom exclaimed, shaking her head, "You are loved! And wonderfully made! And... we're going to talk later, sweet girl. I'm sorry you're having a bad time; Auntie Louise is too. But for the next 10 minutes, you go look up Psalm 139 in the Bible. And make a list of ways God made you wonderful. I don't want to hear you saying those nasty things about yourself."

Gently, she pushed Abigail toward the door. Abigail stomped away to her room, feeling frustrated. What did Psalm 139 have to do with anything? Why would Mom say God made her wonderful?

THUNK. She flipped open the Bible on her desk, being extra loud about it.

Table of Contents, she thought to herself as lots of feelings swirled inside. She found it in the start of her Bible and skimmed her finger down the list of books until she saw "Psalms" and "Page 608" next to it.

FLIP, FLIP, FLIP.

She found page 608, with "Psalms" printed on it in big, pretty letters. Then she flipped slower until she found the big number "139." Just like Mom had said.

SIGH.

Putting her chin in her hands, Abigail bent over her Bible and read. Her heart got softer and softer as she reached the words Mom must have meant…

¹³ "You created the deepest parts
     of my being.
   You put me together
     inside my mother's body.
¹⁴ How you made me is amazing
     and wonderful.
   I praise you for that.
   What you have done
     is wonderful.
   I know that very well.
¹⁵ None of my bones was hidden
     from you
   when you made me
     inside my mother's body.
   That place was as dark
     as the deepest parts
     of the earth.
   When you were putting me
     together there,
¹⁶ your eyes saw my body
     even before it was formed.
   You planned how many days
     I would live.
   You wrote down the number
     of them in your book
   before I had lived through
     even one of them.
¹⁷ God, your thoughts about me
     are priceless.
   No one can possibly
     add them all up.
¹⁸ If I could count them,
   they would be more than
     the grains of sand.
   If I were to fall asleep counting
     and then wake up,
   you would still be there
     with me."

Pulling her Amazing Adventure Box out of her backpack, Abigail took out her multi-pen and clicked down the purple ink button. She always underlined important things in purple. It was one of her four favorite colors.

So... the way God made her was amazing and wonderful?

She took a deep breath. She didn't *feel* amazing and wonderful.

But he knew all about her?

That was what it said—she read the words again. "When you were putting me together there, your eyes saw my body even before it was formed."

So, God knows me... like, really knows me! He knew before I knew me! Abigail realized, trying to imagine how a person could be put together.

"And God is with me," she whispered as she ran her fingers over the part about God still being there even when she fell asleep and woke up. She smiled a little at the idea of God being right there in her bedroom. It made her feel less alone.

Pulling open the drawer of her desk, Abigail

took out her glittery chalk. The walls of her bedroom were covered in big shapes which Mom had painted in special paint that you could draw on. Abigail went right to the tallest shape—a big orange oval. She pulled out a piece of blue chalk and started making her list of things about herself, like Mom had said.

"Well," she said to herself softly, "I guess I can put *amazing* and *wonderful*, since God made me that way."

SCRITCH, SCRATCH.

She wrote it on the wall, and tried to think of anything else good about herself—anything besides the stuff she wasn't good at.

"Hey, Abby," Mom said, poking her head in her room and handing her their tablet. "Auntie Louise is ready now... and so is Evangeline! They're on video. You have a little time while I go start making dinner. We'll talk about your list soon, okay?"

Mom gave her a soft smile as she handed Abigail the tablet.

"Auntie Louise? Evangeline?" Abigail asked, holding it up. "Hello?!"

"Abby!!!" Evangeline exclaimed as her round, smiley face and blonde pigtails showed up on the screen. Evangeline was just a couple years younger than Abigail, but not nearly as little as Henry.

"Hey girl!" Auntie Louise said. Half of her dark hair and warm, smiling face came in sight, until Evangeline leaned in even closer and filled up the screen.

"Where are you?" Evangeline asked, squinting.

"In my room," Abigail explained enthusiastically. She turned the camera around to show them her walls, since they hadn't visited since Abigail's family moved. "This is my Adventure Central!"

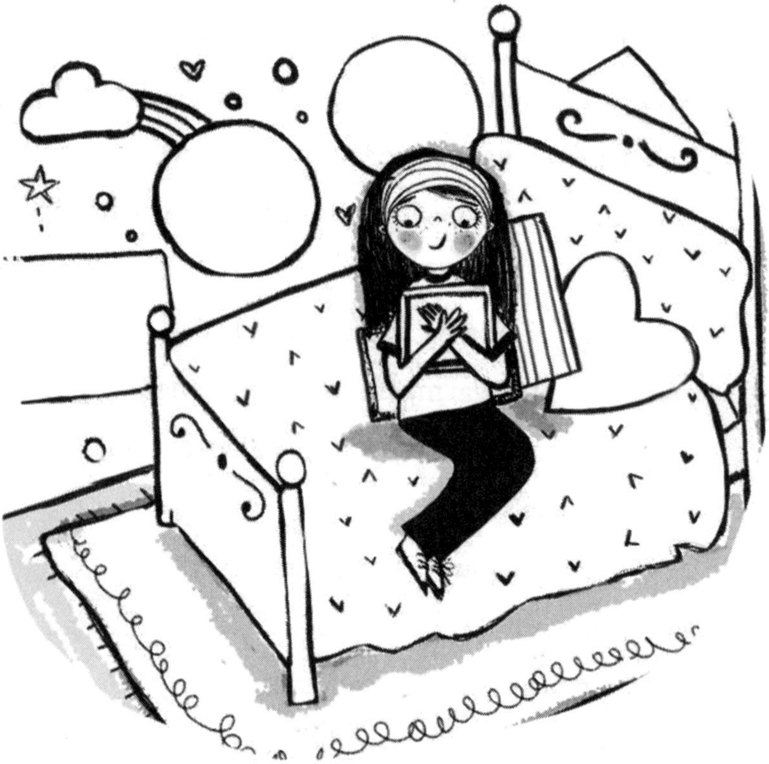

Chapter Eleven

The List

"Ooo, what's that?" Evangeline asked, pointing all over so that Abigail couldn't tell what she meant. "And that?!"

"She means the shapes on your wall," Auntie Louise explained, chuckling.

"They're chalk-paint shapes I can write and doodle and invent in," Abigail grinned, moving the camera nice and close so they could see better.

"Wo-won, won-der…" Evangeline began to sound out what Abigail had written in the orange oval. "It says, *Wonderful!*"

"And *Amazing!*" Auntie Louise added. "Is it the start of a story?"

"No," Abigail explained, turning the camera around so they could see her. "I was reading about how the way God made us is wonderful and amazing. Mom told me to make a list of how God made me wonderful. But I can't think of much…"

"But you're Abby," Evangeline said, looking confused as she squinted again like she was checking to make sure she was really looking at her cousin.

Abigail smiled sadly. "Yeah, but… I can't sing. Not well. Or dance. Or do anything for musicals, or do a real front-roll tumble or… well, I'm terrible at math and… sometimes I just feel like…"

As she trailed off, she saw Evangeline's lip curl all the way down, looking sad for her.

"Sometimes we all feel bad about ourselves," Auntie Louise said softly, "but you know what? God made you on purpose to be loved by Jesus. That makes you pretty special."

"Yeah," Evangeline added, glancing up at Auntie Louise happily before nodding and saying very determinedly, "Jesus loves you!"

PING! A little lightbulb went off in Abigail's mind as she looked from the loving faces of Auntie Louise and Evangeline to her open Bible. She remembered Miss Shanner's words about John 15—Jesus is THE friend who loves perfectly! And that made her… a person loved by Jesus.

"You know what?" Abigail said, smiling back at her aunt and cousin. "You're right. I'm going to put that on my list."

SCRITCH, SCRATCH.

She added "Loved by Jesus" to the list on her wall, after propping up the tablet so they could see her writing in the chalk-paint shape.

"Put *Great adventure girl* on there too," Auntie Louise said, before reminding Evangeline about how Abigail had made up adventures for her the last time they'd seen each other. "And put *Good artist* too."

SCRITCH, SCRATCH, SCRITCH…

Abigail turned back to the camera, worrying a little about how quiet they'd gotten. They were still there! But Auntie Louise was whispering in Evangeline's ear.

"And *Great cousin* too," Evangeline added excitedly, her eyes wide as Auntie Louise pulled away, "who we're coming to see soon!"

"Really?!" Abigail squealed, all her worries falling away in the excitement. She could almost feel one of Auntie Louise's big hugs and Evangeline's hand grabbing hers to tug her outside to play.

"Yes!" Auntie Louise grinned. "For Christmas!"

"YAY!" Abigail cheered, and Evangeline joined right in, jumping up and down.

"Your mom and I just sorted it out," Auntie Louise explained. "It was just what I needed today too."

That reminded Abigail—Mom had said Auntie Louise was having a bad day too. Maybe Abigail should be cheering Auntie Louise up, the way talking to her and Evangeline had cheered Abigail up.

"For Christmas," she said eagerly, "I'll

make lists for each of us of how God made us wonderful. It can even be a game or something!"

Her mind filled with images of game boards and prize wheels and cards as she tried to think up how to make Mom's list idea into something awesome for everyone.

"Yay!" Evangeline repeated, jumping up and down again.

"That's so fun and happy, it helps cheer me up even more!" Auntie Louise smiled. "You should put *Good helper* on your list too, Abby."

KNOCK, KNOCK.

Mom pushed open the door and waved hi into the camera as she stepped next to Abigail.

"I can't wait to be together," Auntie Louise said. "Abby's going to make us all lists for Christmas, like this one you've asked her to make."

"That's a great idea," Mom grinned, giving

Abigail a squeeze and looking at her list on the wall. "*Loved by Jesus*? I love that!"

"Auntie Louise and Evangeline gave me the idea after I read Psalm 139," Abigail said.

"Psalm 139?" Auntie Louise asked. "That's one of my favorites!"

"I think it's one of my favorites now too," Abigail smiled back, happy to have even more in common with her aunt.

"And mine," Mom said, rambling on cheerily. "And Abby, you know another reason why the way God made us is wonderful? He made each one of us to be like him. And at the same time, he made each one of us unique—different than everybody else! So we can all love and care for others in different ways. And Jesus will be with us and help us as we do!"

Auntie Louise chuckled. "Amen to that. Thanks for cheering me up, both of you. And Abby, don't forget to add *Good helper* to that list. Just like God. He's THE BEST helper."

And Jesus is THE BEST friend, Abigail remembered, smiling wide.

"I can't wait for us to celebrate God's goodness together for Christmas!" Mom said, looking like she wanted to hug Auntie Louise through the tablet.

"Yes!" Abigail smiled, feeling like all her bad feelings and worries had been erased by so much love. *Thanks, God,* she prayed inside, *for Mom and Evangeline and Auntie Louise, and thanks for*

being the best helper and the best friend.

As soon as they hung up, Abigail added *Good helper* to her list as Mom watched.

"I'm sorry again that you had a bad day, sweet girl," Mom said gently. "And I'm sorry you were feeling bad about yourself. Remember, God loves you just the way he made you, and so do I. And Dad. And Henry. And Evangeline, and Auntie Louise, and lots of people."

"I know," Abigail grinned.

"You don't have to be good at everything," Mom assured her. "Leave that to God! You just be you and ask God to help you with loving other people like he does, in the wonderful, unique way he made you. Even if you're feeling self-conscious, okay? He will help you, don't worry."

⭐ Chapter Twelve

Uninvited

Skipping down the hallway at school the next day, Abigail sang in her head the words she'd made up to the tune of "The Future," the song from *Frannie*, the night before.

> *I'm a good helper,*
> *always like to help people,*
> *it's just my way!*

She turned into her classroom, full of hope that they would like her ideas for helping—like helping pick out the costumes! Or, maybe she could help with decorating the stage. Her Uncle Ross and Cousin Cameron had done that for Gracie's musical that summer. And Abigail thought she would be good at that sort of thing. No singing, dancing, or being on stage needed! And she'd have a good relationship with the musical girls using her wonderful, amazing skills from God!

So, where were they?

Looking around, she sang inside.

> *Just tell them about*
> *my helping,*
> *then they'll want me*
> *to come help them!*

"Hi!" Abigail called out to Brianna, Maggie, and Flora as soon as she saw them at the back of the classroom. She sang more in her head as she saw the girls start whispering together when she walked toward them. Ooh, a secret!

She couldn't wait to be in on it too.

> *Wonderful, wonderful,*
> *I'm wonderfully made,*
> *It's God's special way today!*

"Hi," Flora, Maggie, and Brianna answered, all together, when she got near them. It was almost like they'd rehearsed speaking in unison as well as singing. They were lined up in a row, too.

"So, have you been practicing?" Abigail asked, hoping they'd say yes and then ask what she'd been doing, so she could share her ideas.

"We have," Maggie said, posing to show off the shiny black shoes on her feet and flouncing the skirt of the red dress she was wearing.

Flora did a little tip-tap jig in a pair of white shoes Abigail had never seen her wear before.

Brianna copied her, finishing with a wave down to her shiny, sparkly heels. Heels!

They were short ones, but still. How did she balance?!

"So, you've got some shoes for the performance, huh?" Abigail asked, trying not to look down at her sneakers, jeans, and slightly wrinkled top. Those weren't fit for a stage! But, she reminded herself, she didn't have to be dressed up. Like Mom said, God had made her on purpose, and she might not be a performer—but she was a helper. And she did have ideas for costumes for the other three! "I was thinking, maybe I could help…"

"Well…" Maggie said, pausing to straighten her red skirt, as if it had been wrinkled by just looking at Abigail's outfit.

"I was thinking," Abigail continued, suddenly feeling nervous about the way they were all standing lined up, so synced together. "I know my tumble idea wasn't a big help, and I missed out on most of your practicing yesterday, but you did make me the director, so I could help with, um, costumes, and decorations, and, um... anything else you want help with?"

"Well..." Brianna echoed Maggie, shooting a glance sideways at Flora.

"Chica," Flora explained, spreading her hands out like she always did when she presented something, "you've been a wonderful director. Thank you! From the bottom of our hearts! But we don't need your help today, and we have a lot of practicing to do since Mrs. Hennig asked us to perform next week, and we know this isn't really your thing, and so, you feel free to go do something that IS your thing!"

BAM.

Abigail felt like her jaw had hit the floor. Like Flora had punched her! Even though she'd only used words. Words that sounded suspiciously practiced.

"Something that is my thing?" Abigail asked,

tucking both hands under her chin like she needed to lift her jaw back up to even speak. "But... helping is my thing. I'm a helper, like God is..."

"I meant your thing like making an Amazing Adventure!" Flora grinned like she didn't realize she'd just hurt Abigail's feelings horribly. "Or creating a story!"

"Something with that sparkly box thing you always play with, you know," Maggie butted in, gesturing to the glittery purple pencil case in Abigail's hands.

"You're very good at that," Brianna concluded, as if she were the expert on what Abigail was and wasn't good at.

Flora just stood there, still smiling.

"I... I..." Abigail began. She didn't know whether she was about to cry or shout. She was being uninvited from the whole musical! From even helping! Just when she finally felt like she had some good ideas! *God,* she cried out inside, *I know you made me and love me! So why don't they? Why don't they want me?*

RINNNGGG!

As the bell cut through the awkward silence, Abigail suddenly felt certain about one thing.

She did NOT want anything to do with the musical—or the musical girls—anymore!

Maybe not even Flora.

Chapter Thirteen

All Alone

Lingering at the back of the line as they stepped out of the doors for recess, Abigail watched Brianna, Maggie, and Flora skip off, arm in arm.

She heard Greg call out, "Tackle tag time!" as he led a bunch of kids off to the farthest part of the field.

Some other classmates giggled on their way to the swing set. But there were five of them, and only five swings.

Looking around to see if there was anyone

else to play with, Abigail spotted a big tree and figured she could hide behind it so no one would see she was all alone.

"Hello, want to be friends?" she sighed as she walked up to the tree. "You'll be my only friend today. And you're not even real."

She patted the trunk, holding herself steady as she peered around the tree to the left and then the right. Good! No one could see her!

"Well, you're real, but not a person," she whispered to the tree.

She turned around and sat down, using the tree trunk as a back rest. Sighing, she fidgeted with her Amazing Adventure Box. Even though she knew it wouldn't make her feel better, she wanted to open it up and write a whole stack of sticky notes, telling her sad story!

She'd write about having been left out more and more, and how she'd braved embarrassment and gotten over her self-consciousness and tried to help, only to be uninvited entirely and left all alone. And how her very best friend had abandoned her! *That* had made her "yesterday and today" "sad and sorry," like it said in the song the girls had picked.

UGH.

That song she just wanted to forget about was stuck in her head.

> *I just look up ahead*
> *And smile and sing, oh,*
> *The stars'll shine*
> *In the future!*

Looking up ahead, all Abigail saw was some empty, grassy space and the wall of her school. Not anything hopeful. Not any friends. Not anyone who would make her feel less lonely.

Leaning her head

back on the tree, she looked up through its leaves. There weren't any stars shining, because it was daytime. But feeling some warm, happy sunshine on her face helped a little. She closed her eyes as the brightness made her squint.

Dear God, she prayed, *thanks for sunshine. Thanks for making me just the way you made me. Even if no one wants to be with me right now. I am a helper, and umm… I'm creative. I bet… I bet I can find some fun, even all alone.*

She looked down and opened up her Amazing Adventure Box determinedly. **ZIP!**

She took out her sticky-note stack and multi-pen.

Glancing up again, thinking, she imagined the tree bending down its branches to say, "Let's have fun! I'm here!"

DING DING DING! That was an idea! Taking a light pink sticky note and pressing it against the bumpy tree bark, Abigail scribbled all over to see what kind of pattern it made. Maybe she could turn the patterns into pictures! Maybe she could pretend they were secret messages! Maybe she could make up a really cool, awesome story of a lonely tree befriending a lonely girl!

SVOOOT. The pen made a noise as she scribbled and scribbled against the tree trunk. She tugged off the sticky note and squinted really closely. *What's the secret message?* she thought, hoping to imagine something cool.

"What's that?" a voice suddenly asked.

Greg. Abigail groaned inside. He'd caught her hanging out with a tree. What was he going to joke now? That she was a sturckle root or something?

"It's the tree pattern," she explained as confidently as she could, relieved that she hadn't accidentally called it a secret message or something else silly. Greg would definitely make fun of that.

"If you used a mix of colors," Greg commented, "it would look cooler. I've seen my mom use cards with colorful patterns like that."

"Oh," Abigail said, holding it out away from herself and looking again. Greg was right—the tree pattern did look pretty cool! And it would be prettier with multiple colors. "Thanks!"

"Hey, what are they doing?" Greg asked, peering around the tree and pointing. Abigail looked and saw Flora, Brianna, and Maggie practicing.

"Practicing their song and dance for the performance on Monday," Abigail began to explain, trying not to look glum.

"HA!" Greg said in a silly high-pitched voice as he stood on his tiptoes and did a mocking little dance. "They look so ridiculous!"

"Well," Abigail began, trying to decide if she should argue it or not. Did she really want to defend them after they'd uninvited her? But did she really want to let Greg make fun of them?

"Shhh," Greg interrupted, peering past her and the tree. "Don't give up my hiding spot, Sturckle. I'm winning tackle tag!"

THUD, THUD, THUD.

Abigail heard running feet, and so did Greg. In a flash, he was gone.

"Well, tree," she whispered to it again, feeling more hopeful, "let's try again." But not for a secret message this time. Greg had given her an idea.

Reaching into her Amazing Adventure Box,

Abigail grabbed the blank cards from kids' club that she'd stashed away in there. With all her upset feelings, she'd forgotten to do anything with them.

One by one, she took them out and pressed them against the trunk, scribbling over their blank covers with different colors to make cool patterns. They looked like something fancy you'd find in a special party store. That would cheer up the lonely old people, wouldn't it? It was cheering *her* up!

RINNNGGG!

Before Abigail knew it, she was running back

to line up for the end of recess, her Amazing Adventure Box full of beautiful, happy cards. They were bright, and unique, and Flora would—

Flora. Abigail sighed, hearing Flora's giggle as she ran up behind her. Normally she'd show Flora her artwork and love hearing her friend's encouragement. Flora was a big fan of Abigail's creative ideas usually. But today...

"Chica!" Flora said happily, tapping her shoulder as she lined up behind her, "Did you do your thing? With your Amazing Adventure Box? We did our thing—just wait till you see us on Monday. It will be FAB-U-LOUS! I'll give you a sneak peek tomorrow..."

CLANNNG.

Mrs. Hennig ushered them inside, which meant it was time to be quiet. But Abigail's heart was noisy with lots of different feelings.

She'd forgotten that Flora was coming over

tomorrow for their regular playdate. Now she didn't know what to do.

She wanted Flora to love the cards she'd created—but she didn't want to show them to a friend who hadn't even realized she'd hurt Abigail's feelings so badly.

She wanted Flora to include her—but she also wanted to uninvite Flora from something so she'd know how it felt.

She wanted Flora to give her a special secret sneak peek of the musical number—but she never wanted to talk about the musical again.

Having good relationships was *hard*.

Chapter Fourteen

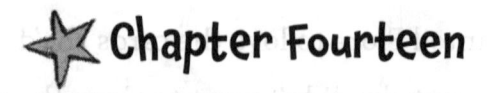

The Very Best Friend

"Abby?" Dad called out when she walked in the door after school. "In here!"

"Hi, Dad," she said, walking into the living room to find him sitting on the couch next to Henry. She hoped they could do something fun so she could forget all about Flora and Brianna and Maggie.

BANG! BASH! WHEEEE! BOOM!

Henry was narrating loudly as he aimlessly

pressed buttons and wiggled a video-game controller. He wasn't old enough to know what he was doing, but somehow the monkey on the screen was running around grabbing bananas and stars without being caught by an alligator.

"Wha—?" Abigail asked, forgetting her mixed-up feelings for a moment as she stared at the super-skilled monkey in amazement. "Dad? How is Henry...?"

"... so good?" Dad laughed, smiling at her and waving at the screen. "It's playing a nice long demo video about how to win the game—but Henry thinks he's the one moving the monkey!"

"Ooooh," Abigail chuckled.

"He always wants to play," Dad explained happily. "I figure this is a good way to include him even though he's not so good at games yet!"

"That's nice of you," Abigail said, looking at the joy on her baby brother's face as he aimlessly pushed buttons and exclaimed, "Pow! Yay! Wheee!"

"No one likes to be left out, right?" Dad shrugged, smiling at her.

Abigail felt a sting deep down in her heart. No, nobody liked to feel left out.

SIGH.

"Everything okay?" Dad asked, patting the open spot next to him on the couch.

"Well," Abigail said, "Flora and some other girls have been making a musical at recess, and it's not really my thing. And, well, there's been some other stuff that wasn't my thing either."

"So you got left out?" Dad asked her sympathetically.

"Yeah," Abigail said, catching her breath, "and I know Mom said yesterday that the way God made me is amazing and wonderful, like it says in Psalm 139... and sometimes our friends disappoint us, like Miss Shanner said... but,

Dad, I felt like nobody even noticed me."

"I'm sorry it's been so hard," Dad said, looking sad for her as he gave her shoulder a squeeze. "But did you know, Abby, that someone did notice you?"

"Who?" Abigail asked, wide-eyed. Had Mrs. Hennig been worried about her? Had she called her parents? No, that couldn't be it—Mrs. Hennig had been the one to invite the other girls to do the musical stuff. Had someone else noticed her and thought she seemed sad? But no one had really seen her when she was super left out. She'd been behind her new tree friend!

Had the tree…? No, that was just silly!

"Jesus noticed you," Dad said softly.

"Oh. Because… he's always with me?" How could she have forgotten that?

"Yes," Dad said, grinning a little. "Do you know that God is your friend? There's a great Bible passage about that."

Reaching for their family Bible next to the couch, Dad began flipping through it.

Henry kept playing his game nice and loud while he did.

WHAM! POW! BOOM!

"Aha," Dad said, tapping a spot in the Bible like he'd found treasure, before sliding it onto

Abigail's lap. "Got it! John chapter 15, verses 12 to 14."

Hey, Abigail thought to herself, *I think that was the memory verse for kids' club!*

> [12] Here is my command. Love one another, just as I have loved you. [13] No one has greater love than the one who gives their life for their friends. [14] You are my friends if you do what I command.

Abigail read the verses out loud and looked at Dad. Why was he smiling so big?

"Jesus loves us SO much," Dad explained, "he gave up his life because he wanted to make people his friends—friends of God! So what are we?"

"We're... we're friends of God!" Abigail answered.

"So we're never alone or unnoticed by God," Dad said. "Isn't that such good news?"

"Yeah!" Abigail agreed, trying to smile but finding her face falling into a frown instead. The verse said that she was supposed to try to be a good friend, just like Jesus. But...

"What's wrong?" Dad asked.

"What if I'm *not* a good friend like Jesus?" she blurted out, her feelings coming out in fast, tangled words. "What if I'm not even sure I *want* to be friends with someone anymore because, well, they weren't nice to me and I don't think I can stand it to be nice to them?"

"Oh, Abby," Dad said, his voice getting really gentle, "sometimes we don't want to be a good friend like Jesus, you're right. Usually because our feelings have been really hurt! But guess what? Jesus knows *exactly* what it's like to be a good friend to someone who's hurt you. Remember, he loves us even though we don't deserve it! So he especially wants to help you love *other* people who don't deserve it either."

TAP, TAP. Dad grinned, tapping the open Bible again. "Check this out. God sent you a helper."

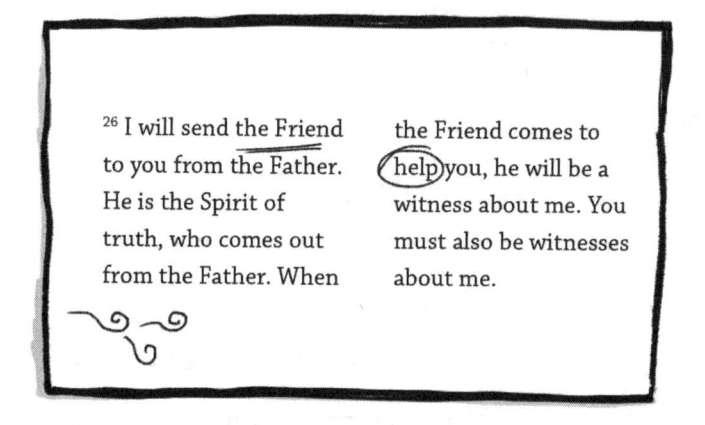

> ²⁶ I will send the Friend to you from the Father. He is the Spirit of truth, who comes out from the Father. When the Friend comes to help you, he will be a witness about me. You must also be witnesses about me.

"Once you've trusted Jesus to be your Savior, the Holy Spirit lives in you," Dad explained as Abigail took a deep breath. "The Spirit reminds you of what's true about Jesus and cares about your hurt feelings, and he'll help you do what God says. Including helping you love other people even when it feels hard to."

WOOO! YAY!

Henry's happy victory noises made it sound like he was excited about that good news.

Abigail was starting to feel excited too.

"So, the Holy Spirit is the Spirit of truth?" she asked, looking at the Bible passage. "And God sent the Holy Spirit to be my friend too? To help me?"

"Yes!" Dad answered happily. "And if anyone knows about friendship, it's God! He is three-in-one! God the Father made you and loves you so much. And he sent Jesus, who loves you so much that he died to save you. And then Jesus sent the Holy Spirit, who loves you so much that he is with you always and helps you always!"

"That is good news," Abigail smiled.

"He's SUCH a good friend," Dad added, smiling wide now, "he'll help YOU be a good friend. Even when it's hard!"

POW!

Henry exclaimed super loud as the monkey whirled around and hurled a banana at the alligator on the screen before it finally went dark.

Abigail remembered how she'd felt punched in the heart by the way Flora had hurt her feelings earlier. She remembered how Flora hadn't even noticed the problem, and acted like everything was fine. Could she really be loving to Flora after that? Maybe...

"Thanks, my very best friend, Jesus," Abigail said happily and softly, praying out loud. "Please, please help me be a good friend to Flora and even Brianna and Maggie! And all of us to be good friends to each other, like you!"

"Amen," Dad said, squeezing her around the shoulders before setting the Bible on the coffee table and picking up another game controller. "Now, are you ready to play?"

⭐ Chapter Fifteen

Saturday

"Abby?" Mom yawned in her doorway the next morning. "Nana just called. She's on her way to pick up those cards you finished last night. Do you want to go with her to help deliver them?"

~~AH-AH-AH!~~ Mom yawned loudly. Abigail giggled, sitting right up in bed. She didn't mind mornings—but Mom always did!

"Yes!" Abigail cheered, already feeling like it was going to be a great day. She jumped out of bed, making a happy list in her head.

Time with Nana!

Helping people who feel lonely!

Hang out with Flora, who can still be my best friend!

All with Jesus, my very best friend!

"Someone's in a good mood," Mom commented, yawning again as she closed the door and wandered off. Abigail knew she'd smell coffee brewing any minute. And if Mom was up this early, that could only mean one thing.

Saturday cinnamon rolls!

Abigail added that to the happy list in her head, then tugged on clean clothes, got ready in the bathroom, and raced to the kitchen to gobble up two warm, doughy rolls covered in sticky white frosting and filled with cinnamon.

"Careful not to get any frosting on your pretty cards," Nana said as she arrived and stood behind Abigail in the kitchen. She reached over Abigail's shoulder to admire her colorful cards with the tree-trunk patterns. "How did you do this?"

"A tree helped," Abigail said, giving Nana a silly smile as she swallowed the last bite of cinnamon roll.

"Ah, well, today it's your turn to help," Nana said back, scooping up the cards and reading the message Abigail had written in every single one, last night, after she and Dad talked. "These are just lovely."

"Do you think they will cheer up the old

people?" Abigail asked, raising her eyebrows hopefully.

"Very much," Nana chuckled, "but let's not call them 'old person'. How about 'Here's a card for you, ma'am' and 'Here's a card for you, sir'?"

"Yes, ma'am," Abigail answered, so serious she was silly.

"Are you secretly calling me old?!" Nana teased.

"I'm not-secretly calling you late," Mom interrupted with a laugh. "Go on, you silly girls—I need a nap from getting up so early! And Abby needs to be back in time to hang out with Flora."

GULP.

Abigail felt her silliness sink down to her stomach, where it knotted up a little. She prayed again for the Holy Spirit to help her be a good, loving friend when Flora came over. A good friend like Jesus.

When they got to the car, Nana handed Abigail a basket to put her cards in. It was full of cards already—Abigail wondered if they had all been made by kids from kids' club or whether Nana had done any herself.

"I hope you have a good day," she read out loud, flipping open one of the cards. "Love, Maisie."

"That's a nice one," Nana grinned as she drove.

"I hope you have a good rest of your life," Abigail read as she flipped open the next one, laughing loudly. "Love, Billy."

HA! Nana looked like she might have to pull over as she laughed so hard and so fast that a few tears came to her eyes. "We might have to take that one out—or give it to someone with a good sense of humor!" she said, wiping the tears from her face as her laughter settled down. "I'm sure he meant it the same way as

'Have a good day!', but..."

"Hahaha," Abigail giggled again. "Do you know which one of the old people—erm, ma'ams or sirs—would think it's funny?"

"I think so," Nana smiled. "It depends what kind of mood she's in. Do you remember how I told you that when I visit, sometimes it's very happy, but sometimes it's sad?"

"Yeah," Abigail said, looking out the window as Nana parked in front of a gray building with big, curtained windows you couldn't see inside of very well.

"I think our cards will help make it a happy day, Abby girl," Nana told her, "and I know Jesus is comforting and caring for the people here. But I just have to warn you—sometimes the people here are having a bad day and you won't get to SEE that they are actually happy that you've come to be a friend to them."

"Okay," Abigail nodded nervously, following

Nana as they walked up to a big door and Nana spoke into the little speaker there.

CLICK.

"So," Nana finished as the door unlocked and opened, "you just smile, be kind, and don't worry about it if anyone seems grumpy or like they don't care. Jesus will show them his love through your love, even if you don't see it happening. Okay?"

"Yup," Abigail confirmed, holding tighter to the basket of cards and hoping the Holy Spirit would help her be a good friend to the old people, even if it wasn't easy.

Chapter Sixteen

A Little Cheer

"Well, hello," a nurse with bright pink scrubs and a big, curly afro said, looking at Abigail with a wide smile. "You have a helper today, Lee."

"I do indeed," Nana smiled back. "We have cards to deliver, to bring a little cheer."

"Wonderful! Well, most of the residents who are awake are gathering in the common room for the weekly hymn sing, starting at 9:30," the nurse replied. She looked at Abigail and added,

"Just stick with your nana. Alright?"

"Yes, ma'am," Abigail said, nervously practicing what Nana had told her. She tried to smile, but only one corner of her mouth managed to go up.

"Let's get going," Nana said, putting a reassuring hand on Abigail's back and guiding her down an empty hallway with tiled floors and bright fluorescent lights.

They passed lots of doors, all cracked open just a little. Abigail heard some people snoring. Some were groaning. But as they neared one wide-open door, she heard…

Singing!

LA DI LA DI LA…

"Has the hymn sing started already?" Nana asked an old man in the doorway, as she and Abigail walked into a big room with rows of cushioned chairs and a few old people sitting in them or in wheelchairs. They all faced a large, blank TV screen and a tall old piano.

"Does that sound like a hymn to you?" the old man barked angrily. Abigail wondered if his frown was really that deep or if the wrinkles just made him look madder than anyone she'd ever seen before. "Dolores is just batty. Shush, Dolores!"

Glancing across the room at an old lady who was swaying in her wheelchair as she sang happily, Abigail grimaced. The song didn't have real words. And her voice sounded squeaky like a mouse. It wasn't very nice to listen to. But... this man was being rude and mean. She hoped Nana wouldn't—

"We have a card for you," Nana said to the man. Softly, she suggested to Abigail, "How about one of those smiley-face ones?"

"Ugh." The man leaned back in the chair and frowned even deeper somehow. "It's not my birthday. Or Christmas," he said suspiciously. "You can't trick me."

"This card is just because," Nana reassured him, giving Abigail a nudge on the shoulder.

RUSTLE.

Abigail found a card at the bottom of the stack that had a smiley face on it, and hurried to hand it to the man. She wondered if he might rip it up—he seemed so grumpy!

"Well," the man said. He huffed a little. He didn't open the card. He hardly looked at it.

"Enjoy the hymn sing," Nana told him, grinning even as she steered Abigail away and across the room.

"He wasn't very nice," Abigail whispered up to Nana, walking as slowly as she could. She wasn't sure she wanted to keep meeting the old people!

"Well, Jesus still loves people who aren't nice," Nana answered softly. "Hopefully that man sees that someday, if he doesn't know Jesus yet."

With a hand on Abigail's shoulder, Nana gently steered her—despite her slow steps—right toward...

Right toward Dolores, whom the man had yelled at.

She was still singing like she'd swallowed a bird.

LA LA LA LA...

Dolores didn't stop singing when Nana said

hi. She had her eyes closed and a big smile on her face as she warbled on.

LA DI LA DI LA...

She kept singing when Nana said they had a card for her too, swaying with her eyes still shut.

At Nana's nudging, Abigail pulled out one with a flower on it and waved it at Dolores as noisily as she could. Dolores still didn't look.

RUSTLE. Nana gently tugged Abigail's hand forward, showing her that she could just put it on Dolores' lap.

The singing stopped. Dolores' eyes shot open. She looked down at the card.

"For me?" she asked. Her talking voice was so hoarse, she sounded a little like a frog. She leaned forward, tipping one ear toward Abigail.

"Yes," Abigail said, trying to smile.

"I think she's almost deaf," Nana whispered.

"YES," Abigail said louder, this time nodding and making herself grin. She even gave a thumbs up, just in case Dolores still didn't understand.

"Thank you!" Dolores answered, grinning so wide that Abigail could see she didn't have any teeth! "Thank you!"

Clutching the card to her chest happily, without even reading it, she just smiled on and on, her eyes looking at Abigail even though they didn't seem to quite focus on her face.

"Have a great day," Nana loudly said, placing a hand on Abigail's shoulder again and turning her toward the back of the room, where another old lady sat in a tall chair.

"Why didn't she read the card even though she liked it?" Abigail asked Nana, confused.

"Some won't, at least not right away," Nana explained. "That's okay. Some people want to talk. Others are just very quiet and don't have lots of words left. The Lord knows what they think and feel, though, huh?"

"Yeah," Abigail said, remembering how Psalm 139 said something like that. She was glad that Dolores wasn't really alone, even if she couldn't hear much and didn't seem to talk much anymore. And even if her singing probably scared some people away!

"Now this next lady, I know already," Nana grinned. "She might like Billy's card. If she's with it today, anyway."

A wide lady in a tracksuit sat up straight in her cushioned chair as Nana and Abigail got near her. She adjusted her oversized glasses, arched a wrinkly eyebrow, and said, "Well, what do we have here?"

Chapter Seventeen

Delia

"My granddaughter, Abby," Nana answered the lady in the tracksuit. "How are you today, Delia?"

"Still not dead," Delia laughed, "so, praise God for that. Not that I'd mind just being with him already."

Nana chuckled. "Well, I'm glad to see you."

"I, uh… I have a card for you," Abigail explained.

RUSTLE. She fished Billy's card out of the basket and handed it over.

"A dinosaur?" Delia asked, running her hand over the front of the card and winking at Abigail. "I bet I'm older than it."

She opened the card and read it out loud: "I hope you have a good rest of your life."

Delia let out a loud hoot like an owl and then cackled and cackled, leaning back in her chair as she laughed. **HA HA HA!**

"Lordy," she said, "that about *made* the rest of my life."

"Thought you'd like it," Nana chuckled.

"Do you know this Billy?" Delia asked Abigail seriously.

"Yeah," Abigail answered, giggling as she began to explain. "He always wants everything to be a game, and to win…"

"Tell him he won Delia's prize for the funniest card ever," Delia said. Then she glanced toward the doorway and called out to a lady who was entering the room: "Agnes! Back here! Come see this card!"

Abigail smiled as Nana steered her away again, thinking how glad Billy would be. Although he probably hadn't meant to be funny! As long as he won, he wouldn't mind.

"Alright, just to warn you," Nana whispered, "this next man is extra lonely. His wife died a few weeks ago." She pointed toward an old man leaning on the back wall.

"That's sad," Abigail said, as she imagined him looking around for someone to talk to and laugh with and hug, like her grandparents were always doing together.

"How's the garden club going?" Nana asked the man, looking at the window he was staring through. Abigail saw that just outside, there were flowers and pretty trees around a small fountain.

"She loved to tend the garden," the man answered, as if they would know who he meant. Abigail figured he must mean his wife who had died.

"Do you like trees?" Nana asked, looking like she already knew the answer.

"Oh, yes," the man said, still looking out the window. Abigail wondered if he thought he might find his wife again if he looked hard enough.

"We have the perfect card for you," Nana said, nodding at Abigail.

RUSTLE.

Abigail began to look for a card with a tree on it—and then she realized. Nana meant one of the cards *she* had made! But would this man be able to tell what the pattern was?

Handing him the card, Abigail glanced

worriedly at Nana.

"Ah," the man said, holding the card up in front of his big glasses and squinting. "Is this... is this the bark of an oak tree?"

"I think so," Nana said encouragingly.

"So nice," the man repeated, opening the card and holding it even closer to his glasses to read it. "Oh, oh, oh."

"We're praying for you," Nana told the man, giving Abigail a side hug as she said it.

"Oh, thank you," the man said, pulling his glasses away from his face to swipe tears away. "I'm so lonely since she died, but you know... I... I know Jesus is with me. 'I have called you friends,' he said—do you know that verse? It's my favorite verse in the Bible. John 15, verse 15. I just needed the reminder. Thank you!"

"John 15?" Abigail asked. Inside her heart, she thanked God. That was the chapter she and Dad had looked at! And the kids'-club memory verse was from John 15 too! The Holy Spirit must be helping this man remember Jesus' love, just like Dad said. What a good friend God was!

"That was pretty cool," Nana said as she steered Abigail away to sit down by the piano. "God knew just what would be special to that man, didn't he?"

"Yeah," Abigail smiled. Inside, she added, *And you knew it would be special to me too, huh, God? Thank you! Thank you for being such a loving friend!*

The hymn sing was starting. Abigail heard the voices of Delia and her friend Agnes, and even the grumpy old man she'd met when they first walked in! Dolores was still hugging her card and singing "La, la, la." Between that and the loud piano, Abigail wasn't embarrassed to join in the singing too—no one would be able to hear that she wasn't very good!

Then the words to the second song came up on the TV screen in front of them.

> What a friend we have in Jesus,
> All our sins and griefs to bear!
> What a privilege to carry
> Everything to God in prayer!

Abigail knew she DEFINITELY couldn't stay quiet for this one!

Chapter Eighteen
Three Surprises

"I think it's wonderful that God made music the way he did," mused Nana as she drove Abigail home. "It just reaches right to my heart and cheers me up every time! Hymns, musicals... it doesn't really matter what type of music it is! It's one of the ways God gives me joy."

HMMM. Abigail thought about the songs they'd just sung—especially the one about Jesus being her friend. That one made her happy! Then she thought about the musical at school and remembered how that song and dance made Flora and the girls so happy… and she remembered how Mom had told her that God made people unique, to show others things about him.

Maybe… maybe Flora's love of musical stuff was part of how God had uniquely made her. To bring people joy.

So maybe… maybe she could encourage Flora in that, even if the musical stuff wasn't Abigail's thing?

CRUNCH. They pulled onto the gravel driveway, and Nana fluttered her hands like she was dancing, to say goodbye.

"Have fun with Flooooora!" Nana sang-said with a smile before pulling away.

"I hope so," Abigail whispered to herself as she turned to go inside. The words to the song about Jesus being her friend and carrying things to him in prayer kept playing in her head. *God,* she prayed, *please, help me to love Flora like you love me! Please help me to be a good friend even if musicals aren't my thing! Please help me to forgive her for hurting my feelings without even knowing it!*

CLICK, CLICK. She turned the doorknob and walked inside.

"Gabigaa!" Henry exclaimed, running up to her and grabbing her hand. "Shhh!"

"Shhh? Why?" she asked him in a whisper, following as he tugged her toward the kitchen doorway.

"Shhhhhh," Henry repeated, not very quietly.

He tugged her right around the corner to...

"SURPRISE!" Flora yelled, leaping out from behind the table.

"Flora got here before you," Mom smiled at Abigail, whose eyes were wide as she tried to get over being so startled.

"AND," Flora continued, bouncing over to

the freezer with excitement, "I also brought a surprise! It's DOUBLE surprise day!"

"Ice cweam!" Henry cheered, spoiling the surprise—but only by a few seconds.

"Mama got ice-cream sandwiches—the kind with rainbow candies in them," Flora explained, happily pulling three little blue packages out of the freezer. "I begged her to let me bring some for you and Henry too. I know you love these! Surprise!"

"This is so nice of you!" Abigail exclaimed, gleefully taking hers and sitting down at the table to eat it before it began to melt.

Ice cream wasn't so good when it was melty, but Abigail's heart had started to feel gooey in a good way. She hadn't expected Flora to think of something nice for her, or to be really thinking of her at all after she'd been so caught up with Maggie and Brianna all week.

"Of course!" Flora grinned, tearing her package open to start eating too. "You're my best Chica!"

Abigail wondered if Flora knew she was giving her a third surprise by being so kind—the best one yet! She put down her ice cream, leaned over, and gave her friend a gigantic hug.

CRINKLE...
DRIP.

"Nummy nummy," Henry said from the floor, his face somehow already covered in ice cream and dripping all over.

"How did you...?" Flora began to ask, her jaw hanging open in amazement that he had eaten so quickly—and had made a mess that fast too!

"It's his special skill," Mom laughed, wiping ice cream off the floor. "And my special skill is clean up—he'll be going to the B-A-T-H after one last super-speedy Henry bite."

"He doesn't like B-A-T-H-S," Abigail explained, spelling out the word too as she took a tidy bite of her tasty treat.

"Haha," Flora giggled as Henry's ice-cream sandwich disappeared and Mom scooped him up swiftly to disappear too. "So, what's *your* special skill, Chica?"

"Uh," Abigail answered, feeling her stomach lurch. It wasn't because of the ice cream. She'd spent lots of time that week worrying about her special skills—or really, about not having special enough skills—and it was partly because of Flora. But now Flora was being a good friend!

Help me be a loving friend to Flora and not get stuck on all those bad feelings I've had, God! she prayed inside.

"Ooh," Flora continued, "I know! You are a GREAT helper. That's your special skill, right?"

"Right," Abigail agreed.

"And my special skill..." Flora said, pausing to rub her chin dramatically before leaping out of the chair, "is singing! And dancing! And acting! And all things..."

She sang the last part out loud: "Muuuusical!"

Chapter Nineteen
A Brilliant Idea

Abigail smiled. Flora really did love musical stuff—the same way Abigail loved making up stories and games and adventures.

"Except," Flora added, her face falling a little as she set her last bite of ice-cream sandwich down sadly, "I heard Greg is making fun of the musical."

"Greg makes fun of everything," Abigail said, trying to cheer Flora up.

"I know, but..." Flora continued, sighing loudly as she said all at once, "I just wish we could perform for people who would *like* to see us. People like the audience in that movie that we wanted to copy from—they were happy because of the musical. And I just want our song and dance to make people happy."

PING! A jolt in Abigail's mind got her attention. And it wasn't brain-freeze from the ice cream they were eating.

Suddenly she knew *exactly* who would be happy to hear a good song and see a nice dance! She knew a way Flora could give joy to people through music. AND she knew how to help make that happen. That was her super special skill, after all!

"Be right back," Abigail said, jumping up. "I have an idea."

PATTER, PATTER, PATTER.

"Just a minute," Abigail called to Flora from the next room.

PATTER, PATTER, PATTER.

"Here we go," Abigail said as she jogged back to the table with her Amazing Adventure Box and some printer paper in hand.

"Okay, but what are you doing?" Flora asked, watching curiously as Abigail got to work on one of the pieces of paper.

SCRITCH, SCRATCH, SWOOSH.

Abigail drew...

A curly red-head in a fancy dress.

Some fancy shoes on her feet.

Music notes around her head.

"Is that...?" Flora asked, leaning so far over the table to see better that she was practically on top of it.

As quickly as she could, Abigail scrawled:

Frannie: The Future

Starring: Flora, Brianna, and Maggie.

Time: Monday after recess AND next Saturday

Place: Corolla Elementary School and Pringle Nursing home.

"A poster for our performance!" Flora grinned as she read. "Wait... TWO performances?!"

"I think the nursing home my nana helps at would love a song and dance! I was just there today!" Abigail exclaimed.

"A nursing home. Like... where old people live?" Flora asked, raising an eyebrow.

"NANA!" Henry shouted, only understanding that part as he walked back into the kitchen, still wet from his bath.

"Yeah, they like music a lot," Abigail explained hurriedly, "and they're lonely, and some are sad... and my nana says God uses music to bring joy, kind of like the cards we brought there today... And you want the musical to make people happy, so I thought..."

"That. Sounds," Flora interrupted seriously, pausing to be extra dramatic. "Awesome!"

But then she frowned and picked up Abigail's multi-pen. "You forgot something."

"Hmm?" Abigail asked, leaning closer to look at her poster and trying to guess where she'd gone wrong.

Flora clicked the pen to purple, the color they both liked a lot. She wrote right under the girls' names:

Directed by Abby

TA-DA!

"But..." Abigail began, feeling a lump in her throat. "I wasn't a good director."

"Of course you are," Flora smiled. "Me and Brianna and Maggie loved it when you watched us practice when we were still figuring it out. It was so nice of you—we know musicals aren't really your thing, but you really wanted to help!"

Standing up straight like she'd made a decision and Abigail shouldn't argue, Flora spread her hands out and put on her best announcer voice. "Presenting the FOUR friends and their FANTASTIC, happy song and dance: 'The Future' from *Frannie: The Musical*!"

CLAP, CLAP, CLAP! WOO!

Henry was back from his bath already! He joined Flora's clapping, adding in some cheers and shouts just for fun.

"Yessss!" Abigail joined in too, amazed that she meant it. She was excited about the musical now, and about Jesus and helping others and friendship... even friendship with the other girls, not just Flora. Maggie would love how pretty the poster looked. Brianna would love how neat and organized it was! She couldn't wait to hear them be excited too.

⭐ Chapter Twenty

One Week Later

"Ready?" Abigail asked Flora, Brianna, and Maggie one week later, as Nana talked into the speaker by the door of the nursing home.

"Yeah!" Flora cheered, tapping her shiny white shoes excitedly and adjusting the fake glasses she had on her face. "Monday's school performance was pretty good, but we've had more practice now, so this will be GREAT! And this audience won't have any boys laughing at us… I hope!"

"I don't think they'll laugh at us," Maggie

said, looking down at her red dress and smoothing its skirt before she straightened the red curly wig on her head and met Abigail's eyes happily. "Old people are more elegant. I'm so glad you've set this up, Abby."

"I hope it's fine," Brianna added softly, not looking down at her shimmery silver dress or sparkly high heels but staring straight ahead. Abigail couldn't tell for sure, but she thought Brianna might be shaking a little. And it wasn't even cold outside.

CLICK. The door opened, and the girls followed Nana inside quietly.

"Don't worry," said Abigail to Brianna, gesturing at the wide, tiled hallway with fluorescent lights. "It's just like school really."

But Brianna shivered again. "School doesn't smell like someone just cleaned everything from top to bottom!"

"We'll head right to the common room," Nana

said after she'd greeted the lady in pink scrubs at the front desk. "It sounds like the residents have been very excited since I hung up Abby's posters."

"Do you think Dolores will be able to hear us?" Abigail asked Nana as they walked toward the common room. "Will Ms. Delia be there?" she added, remembering the lady in the tracksuit who'd liked Billy's card so much.

COUGH, COUGH.

"What was that?!" Brianna exclaimed, jumping a little at the noise.

"Oh, it's just…" Nana began to say.

GROOOAAAN…

"Ah!" Brianna squeaked, jumping again.

CRASH! She lost her balance and fell down on the tiled floor. One of her shiny high heels popped right off. It bounced away like it was dancing all by itself.

"Are you okay?" Nana asked gently.

"I... I..." Brianna stuttered, "I'm okay, I just... I got spooked."

Her cheeks were red.

Her eyes were wide.

Her words were jumbled.

She's nervous and embarrassed, Abigail thought. *I know how that feels.* But she wondered why. Brianna hadn't seemed nervous performing at school.

"There are quite a few noises here, huh?" Nana said nicely. "It's okay, though. The nurses are taking good care of the people here."

"Uh-huh," Brianna said. But she didn't get up off the floor.

"Should we keep going?" Maggie asked, looking between them all. "I see one of Abby's awesome posters on the door—and I hear talking—and I think there are lots of people in that room! Maybe our audience?!"

"Oh yes, that's the common room," Nana said. "We're almost there."

Brianna let out a deep breath, but she still didn't get up.

"Maybe," Nana suggested gently, "some of us should go ahead, and some of us could take a little break first?"

"Let's go ahead!" Flora cheered, looping her arm through Maggie's and tossing Brianna the high heel that had danced away when she fell.

"You take a few minutes, Brianna. That fall looked scary!"

"Are you coming, director Abby?" Maggie asked, smiling.

"Umm," Abigail said, glancing between the happy, bouncing girls, her Nana's soft smile, and Brianna, sprawled out on the floor. She didn't want Brianna to feel alone, or embarrassed, or left out, or anything like she'd felt last week. "Brianna and I will come in a minute."

"Well, I'd better go ahead then, since these girls don't know anyone," Nana said. She gave Abigail's shoulder a squeeze and then led Maggie and Flora to the common room, their excited chatter trailing behind them.

"So…" Abigail began, looking down at Brianna, who was staring at the gray tiles beneath her and the shoe that Flora had tossed her. It was extra sparkly as it wobbled around in her shaky hands, looking cheerful and fun. But Brianna still wasn't getting up.

Dear God, help me to help her! Abigail prayed. *I want to be a good friend, like you.*

"I... I..." Brianna whispered. "I'm nervous in hospitals and places like this. They creep me out."

"Oh," Abigail answered, looking around at the stark walls and wheelchairs in the hall. How could she show Brianna it wasn't a bad place?

She looked around again and saw... Delia! Perfect!

Chapter Twenty-One
What Friends Are For

"Hi, Ms. Delia," Abigail said.

"Oh, hello," Delia answered. She looked a little confused.

"Brianna, this is Ms. Delia," Abigail said, trying to be polite and hoping that, once Brianna saw how nice and happy some of the people in the nursing home were, she wouldn't be so creeped out.

"Hello," Brianna said, looking up nervously at the elderly woman.

"Are we playing on the floor today? Do I have

to get down there too?" Delia asked. Abigail wondered how she could keep such a straight face! Of course they weren't playing on the floor—how silly!

"We're here for the musical number," Abigail explained cheerfully, "right, Brianna? Here in this nice nursing home, with nice people like Ms. Delia."

"What part am I playing again?" Delia asked.

"Ummm," Abigail said.

"Ummm," Brianna said, finally glancing up to look with confusion at Abigail.

"Del," a tiny old lady said as she left the common room and walked over to where

Brianna still sat and Abigail and Delia stood. "Are you coming? The kids are performing soon."

"The kids?" Delia asked, looking at Abigail and Brianna again as she wrinkled her already wrinkly forehead, looking more confused.

"Don't mind her," the other lady said, taking Delia's arm. "She has good days and bad days, and on the bad days she gets confused sometimes. But we're friends, and I remind her what's true. Isn't that right, Del? This way..."

As Delia was led away, Abigail looked down at Brianna again, trying to figure out what would help her get up.

Please, God, she prayed, *help me love Brianna, even if it makes me look a little silly. Help me tell the truth, like Delia's friend tells her the truth when she needs it.*

PLOP. Abigail sat down on the tiled floor next to Brianna. Right in the middle of the hallway.

Even though she was wearing a nice orange and blue dress Mom had picked out for her.

"I was nervous the first time I came here too," Abigail admitted.

"You were?" Brianna asked, meeting her eyes.

"Yeah," Abigail shrugged, "but it's okay—it turned out pretty great! I'm glad you guys are here with me this time."

"I'm glad *you're* here with *me*," Brianna answered, giving a wobbly grin that made Abigail feel like her heart was taking a deep breath.

"Sorry you're nervous," Abigail said softly.

"It's silly," Brianna shrugged. "Nothing's going to hurt me here, right?"

"I don't think so," Abigail said, smiling reassuringly. "Maybe the sound of the old people singing—some of them are worse than me!"

"Maybe you're not as bad as you think,"

Brianna told her, chuckling. "And if you are, it's okay. You're good at lots of other things, like being a friend."

They grinned at each other. Then they both glanced up at the door ahead—they could hear more and more voices coming through it.

"Should we get going, friend?" Abigail asked, sticking her hand out.

They both giggled as they pulled each other up awkwardly, Brianna still wearing just one shoe.

RUSTLE, RUSTLE.

"There," Brianna said, straightening out Abigail's dress and dusting her off in her usual motherly way before putting her own stray shoe back on. "What now, director Abby?"

"It's time for the show," Abigail answered, leading Brianna into the common room where the audience awaited.

CLAP, CLAP, CLAP!

Flora and Maggie got the whole room

clapping as soon as Brianna and Abigail entered!

"Ready?" Nana asked as she put an arm around Abigail's shoulder and guided her to a seat in the front row, right next to Delia and her friend.

Nodding, Abigail gave Brianna a reassuring thumbs up as she lined up next to Flora and Maggie.

"Now presenting," Flora announced in her most dramatic voice, "The song 'The Future' from *Frannie: The Musical*! Starring me, Flora, and Maggie and Brianna. Directed by our friend Abby!"

Someone behind the piano began to play.

DAH DUM DAH DUM DAH...

The girls started dancing—and as soon as they began to sing, a whole lot of smiling old people joined in!

And so did Nana.

And so did Abigail, smiling wide as her friends performed.

"The stars'll shine
In the future
Bet you everything else
That the future will be bright!
Just dreamin' about
The future
Does away with worries

And the hurting till it's alright.
When yesterday and today
Are sad and sorry,
I just look up ahead
And smile and sing, oh!
The stars'll shine
In the future
So you gotta wait
For the future coming soon.
The future, the future,
I look to the future,
It's just a moment away!
The stars'll shine
In the future
So just wait now
For the future,
It's just a moment away!"

Abigail couldn't not join in. Not when she knew that her future was bright because God had given her lots of people to be a good friend to—and who were good friends to her too!

She hoped they'd stay and sing some hymns,

like that one about Jesus being their friend. She'd sing then too. How could she not sing with joy, knowing that Jesus was her very best friend and made her wonderfully?

He probably even liked her tone-deaf singing!

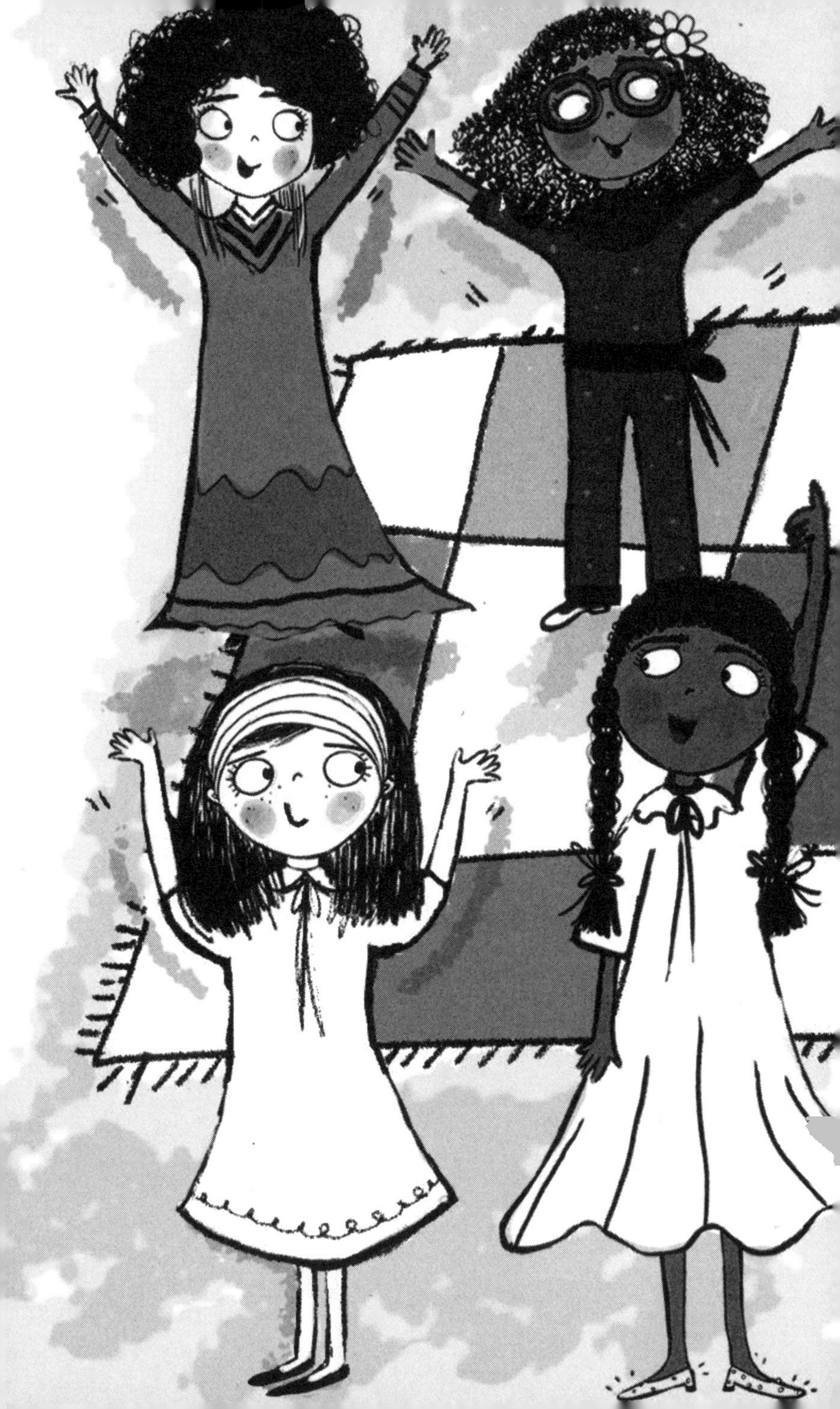

A Note From the Author

Dear reader,

I got along with most kids in school. But I didn't get invited to lots of parties. Many times, I was picked last during sports. And the first time I tried out for a musical, I ended up being the assistant director because I wasn't loud enough to be on stage!

Like Abigail in this story, I've had lots of times when I felt lonely, left out, and like a weirdo. Sometimes it was because someone was being mean to me—but lots of times, it was just that other people fit in, in a way that I didn't.

The truth, like Abigail learns in this story, is that none of our relationships—even the best ones—will be perfect. But there is someone who is perfect and treats us perfectly: Jesus! That means...

1. God knows everything about us, good and bad, and still loves us completely!
2. Jesus frees us from having to worry about if we're loved or understood, because he loves us and understands us!
3. We are never truly alone, because Jesus is with us through his Spirit. He is our good, faithful, forever friend, who we can always count on!

When we follow Jesus, we belong, because he has called us his friends. And that makes us so confident and so secure in him that we can love each other as Jesus has loved us (John 15:12).

When you feel like you don't belong, I pray you'll remember that no matter how you fit in (or don't fit in) with others, you are perfectly known and completely loved by Jesus. And that will never change.

Keep close to Jesus!

Your friend,

Bethany

Wish you could join in with Abigail's games? You can! Visit **abigailseries.com** to find…

Adventure Central

Turtle Tag Instructions

How to Make Encouragement Cards

Bible-Verse Doodle Printouts

Flora's Dictionary of Musical Words

How to Use a Tree to Make Cool Patterns

Worksheets from Abigail's Kids' Club

… and more!

Book-Club Questions

For Chapters 1-2

1. If you were going to pick anything to play with your friends during recess, what would you pick?
2. What do you think the other girls were thinking and feeling as Abigail tried to play musical with them but struggled?
3. Have you ever felt left out? What did you do?

For Chapters 3-5

4. Which answers would you pick for the this-or-that game Miss Shanner led? Would you have much in common with Abigail?

5. Read John 15:12. What makes Jesus' love so perfect? What makes it so hard for us to love others like Jesus does?
6. Miss Shanner explained that Jesus helps us in our relationships with each other. Can you think of ways you need his help in any relationships right now?

For Chapters 6-9

7. If you were trying to find a way to help the musical girls like Abigail was, what would you suggest?
8. Do you think Abigail was understanding Flora's feelings about their friendship correctly? Why or why not?
9. Have you ever been "sturckled" in a situation that wasn't fun or wasn't fair? How did that make you feel?

For Chapters 10-11

10. Why do you think Abigail got so upset when her mom asked her to wait? Do you think she was overreacting?
11. Look up Psalm 139:13-18. What does God know about you?
12. What sorts of things would you put on a list of ways God made you wonderfully? How about if you were making a list for one of your friends or family members?

For Chapters 12-14

13. Why do you think Flora, Maggie, and Brianna didn't want Abigail's help anymore? Do you think they should have found a way for her to help anyway?
14. If you were all by yourself, and Jesus was the only friend with you, what kinds of things would you talk to him about?

15. Look at John 15:12-14 and 26. What makes Jesus such a good friend? Is there any way you want to ask Jesus to help you be a better friend?

For Chapters 15-17

16. Have you ever struggled to know what to say to someone to be a good friend to them? How did you feel?
17. What would you do if you told someone about how Jesus loves them and they didn't like it?
18. What are some of your best ideas for encouraging people and tell them Jesus loves them?

For Chapters 18-21

19. Do you ever get stuck in bad feelings you've had, especially after someone has hurt your feelings? Is there anything you might do differently next time?

20. What do you think changed in Abigail's heart and mind that made her excited about doing the musical number with Flora, Maggie, and Brianna in the nursing home?
21. How did you see Jesus being a good friend to Abigail in this story? How have you seen Jesus being the very best friend to you this week too?

Don't miss Abigail's other adventures!

Book 1: Abigail and the Big Start Over

Book 2: Abigail and the Career Day Catastrophe

Book 3: Abigail Gets Left Out

Keep an eye on **abigailseries.com** for news and updates!

thegoodbook COMPANY

BIBLICAL | RELEVANT | ACCESSIBLE

At The Good Book Company, we are dedicated to helping Christians and local churches grow. We believe that God's growth process always starts with hearing clearly what he has said to us through his timeless word—the Bible.

Ever since we opened our doors in 1991, we have been striving to produce Bible-based resources that bring glory to God. We have grown to become an international provider of user-friendly resources to the Christian community, with believers of all backgrounds and denominations using our books, Bible studies, devotionals, evangelistic resources, and DVD-based courses.

We want to equip ordinary Christians to live for Christ day by day, and churches to grow in their knowledge of God, their love for one another, and the effectiveness of their outreach.

Call us for a discussion of your needs or visit one of our local websites for more information on the resources and services we provide.

Your friends at The Good Book Company

thegoodbook.com | thegoodbook.co.uk
thegoodbook.com.au | thegoodbook.co.nz
thegoodbook.co.in